SNAIL
FINDS A HOME

by MARY PETERSON

ALADDIN PIX

NEW YORK   LONDON   TORONTO   SYDNEY   NEW DELHI

ALADDIN PIX

Simon & Schuster Children's Publishing Division
1230 Avenue of the Americas, New York, New York 10020
First Aladdin PIX hardcover edition March 2020
Copyright © 2020 by Mary Peterson
All rights reserved, including the right of reproduction in whole or in part in any form.
ALADDIN and related logo are registered trademarks of Simon & Schuster, Inc.
ALADDIN PIX and colophon are trademarks of Simon & Schuster, Inc.
For information about special discounts for bulk purchases, please contact
Simon & Schuster Special Sales at 1-866-506-1949 or business@simonandschuster.com.
The Simon & Schuster Speakers Bureau can bring authors to your live event.
For more information or to book an event contact the Simon & Schuster Speakers Bureau
at 1-866-248-3049 or visit our website at www.simonspeakers.com.
Book designed by Karina Granda and Tiara Iandiorio
The illustrations for this book were rendered digitally.
The text of this book was set in Archer.
Manufactured in China 1219 SCP
2 4 6 8 10 9 7 5 3 1
Library of Congress Control Number 2019936831
ISBN 978-1-5344-3185-0 (hc)
ISBN 978-1-5344-3186-7 (eBook)

For Petra, the apple of my eye

—Cookie

CHAPTER 1

Snail lived in an old rusty bucket
full of sweet red strawberries.

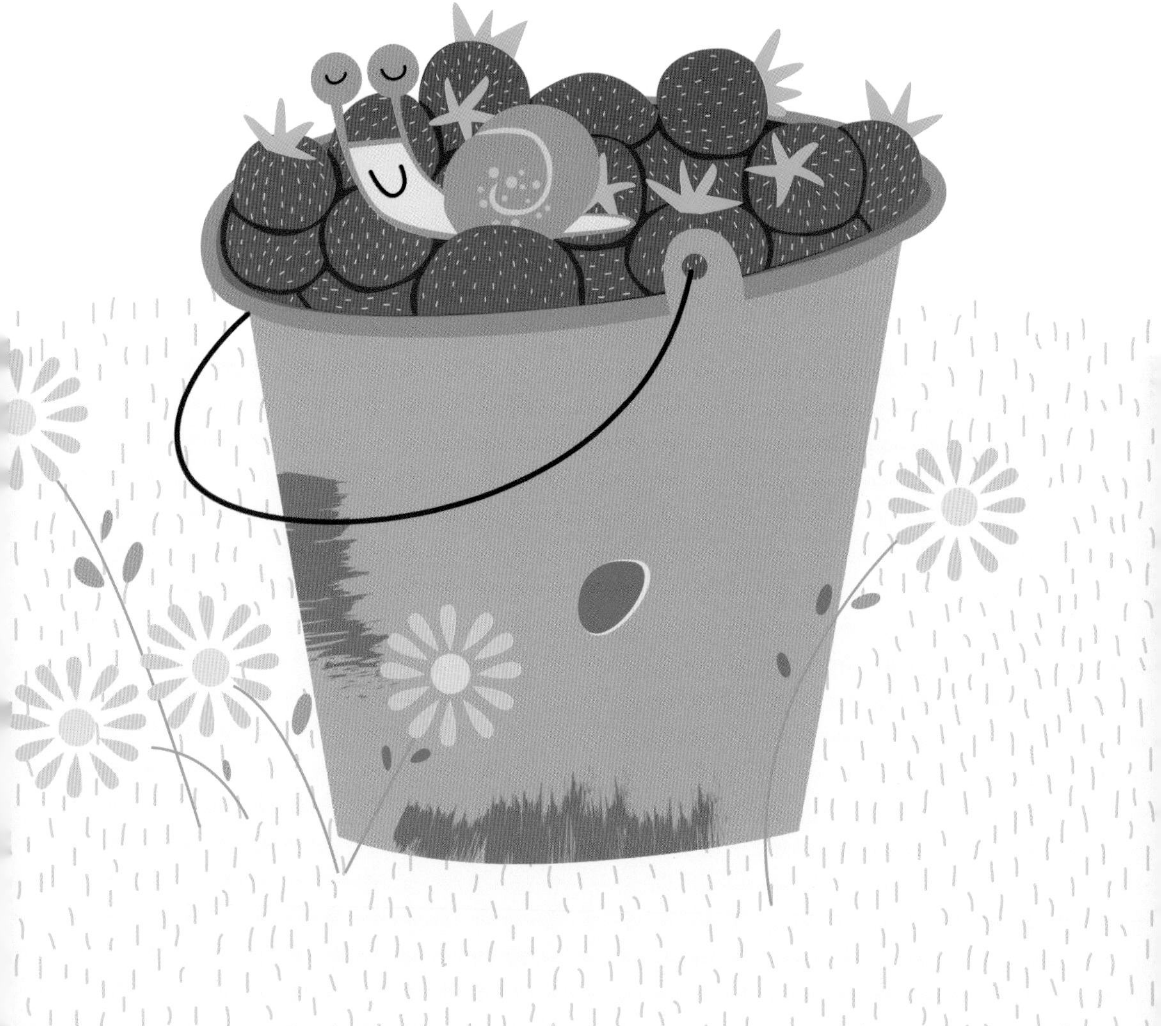

He loved his bucket.

But he loved strawberries even more.
Snail ate strawberries for all his meals.

BREAKFAST

LUNCH

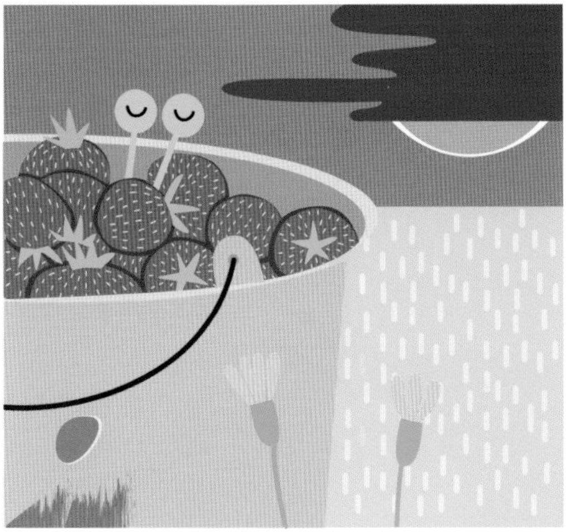

SUPPER

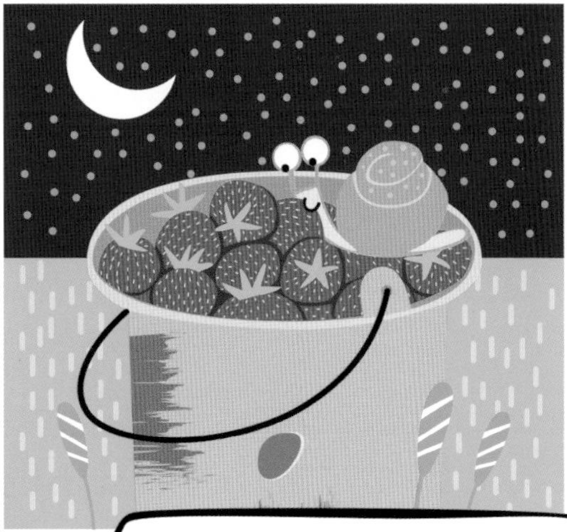

AND DESSERT

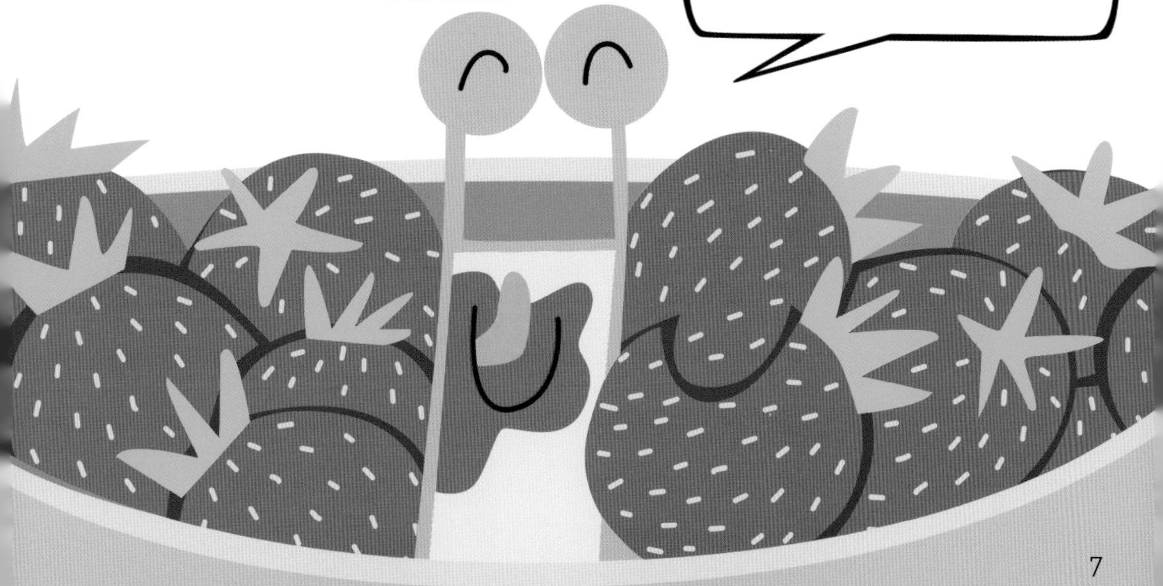
I love SWEET!
RED!
STRAWBERRIES!

Every day, Snail's best friend, Ladybug, came to visit. And every day, she would ask the same question.

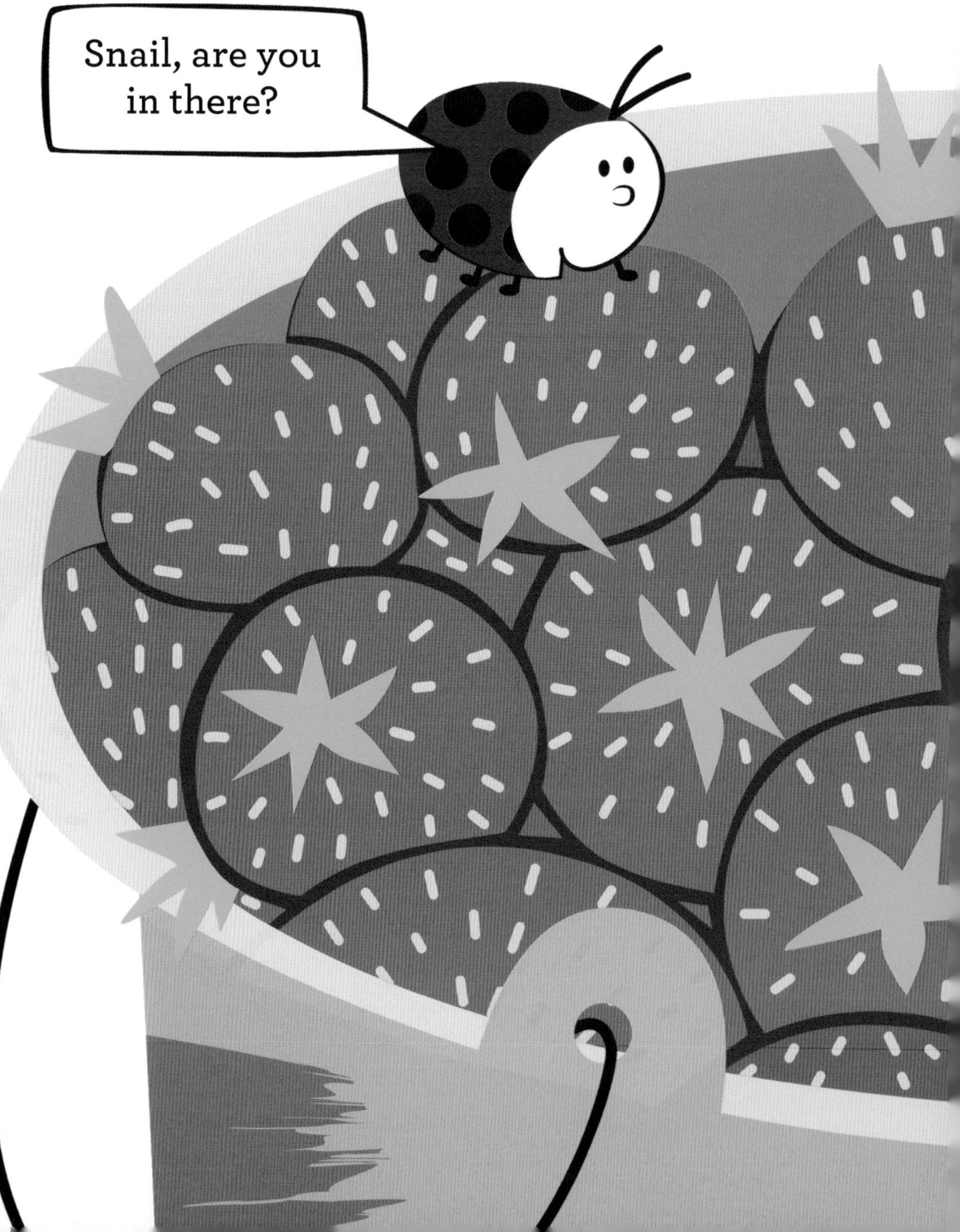
Snail, are you in there?

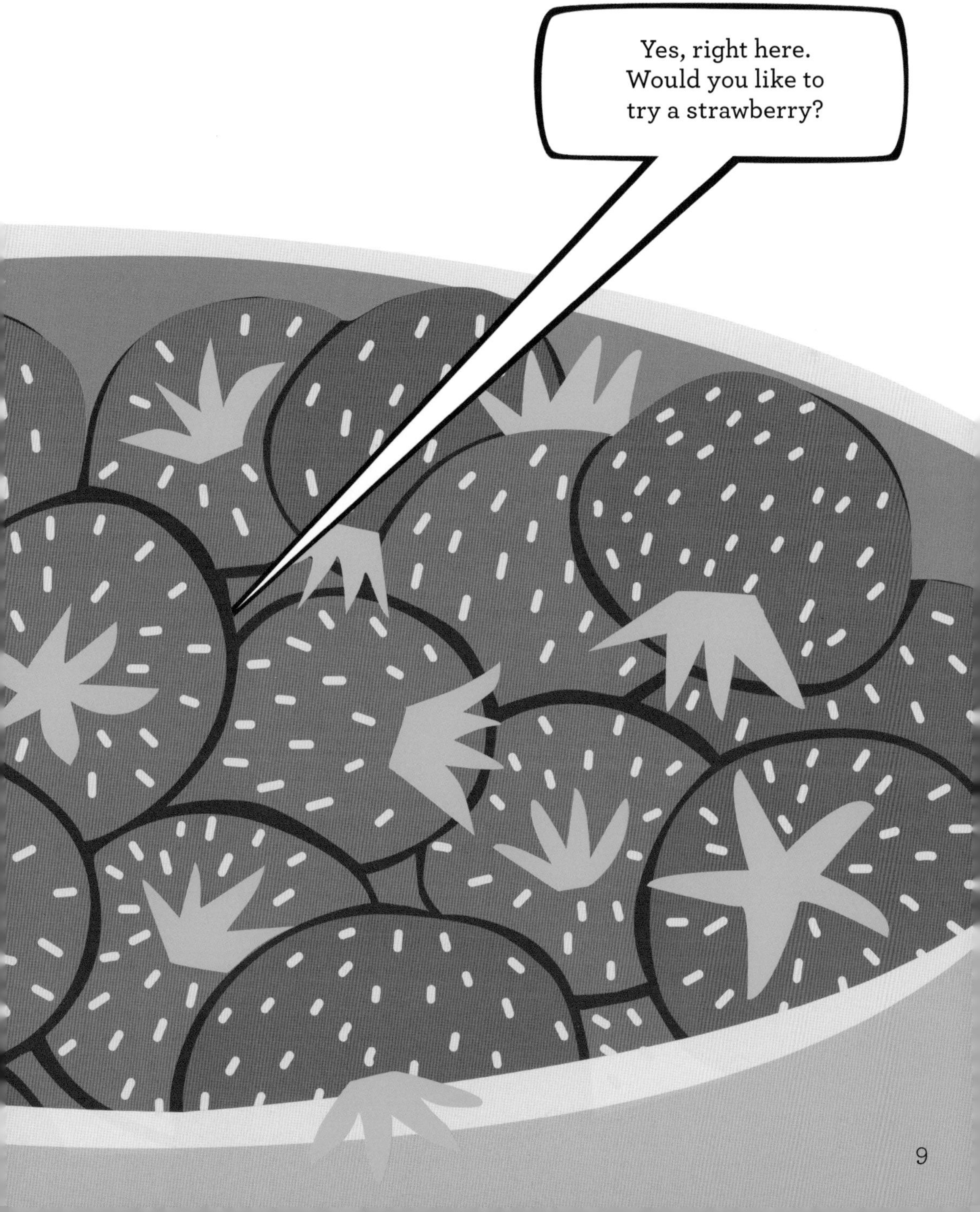
Yes, right here. Would you like to try a strawberry?

Ladybug was always trying to convince Snail that he couldn't live in a rusty bucket eating strawberries forever.

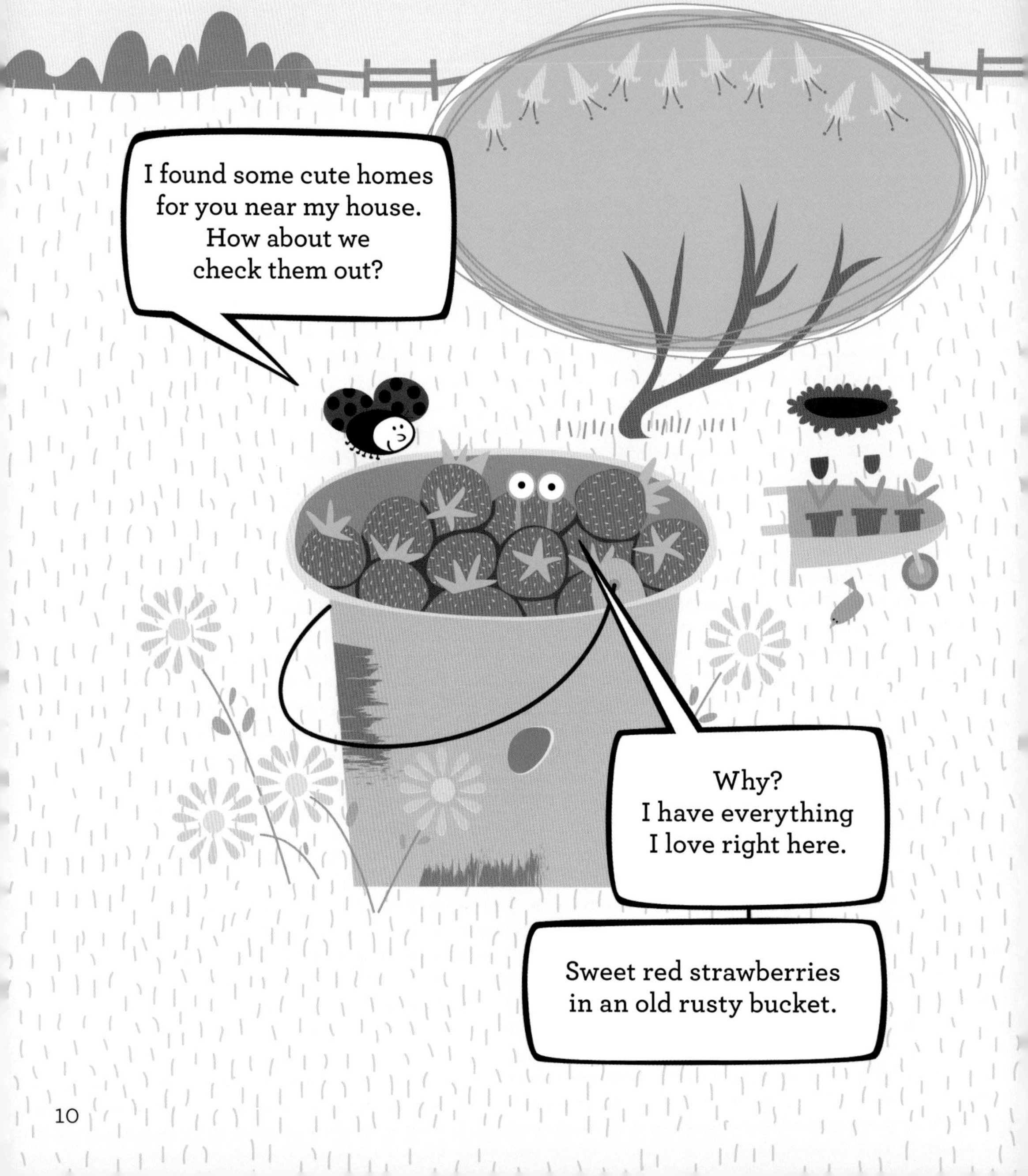
I found some cute homes for you near my house. How about we check them out?
Why? I have everything I love right here.
Sweet red strawberries in an old rusty bucket.

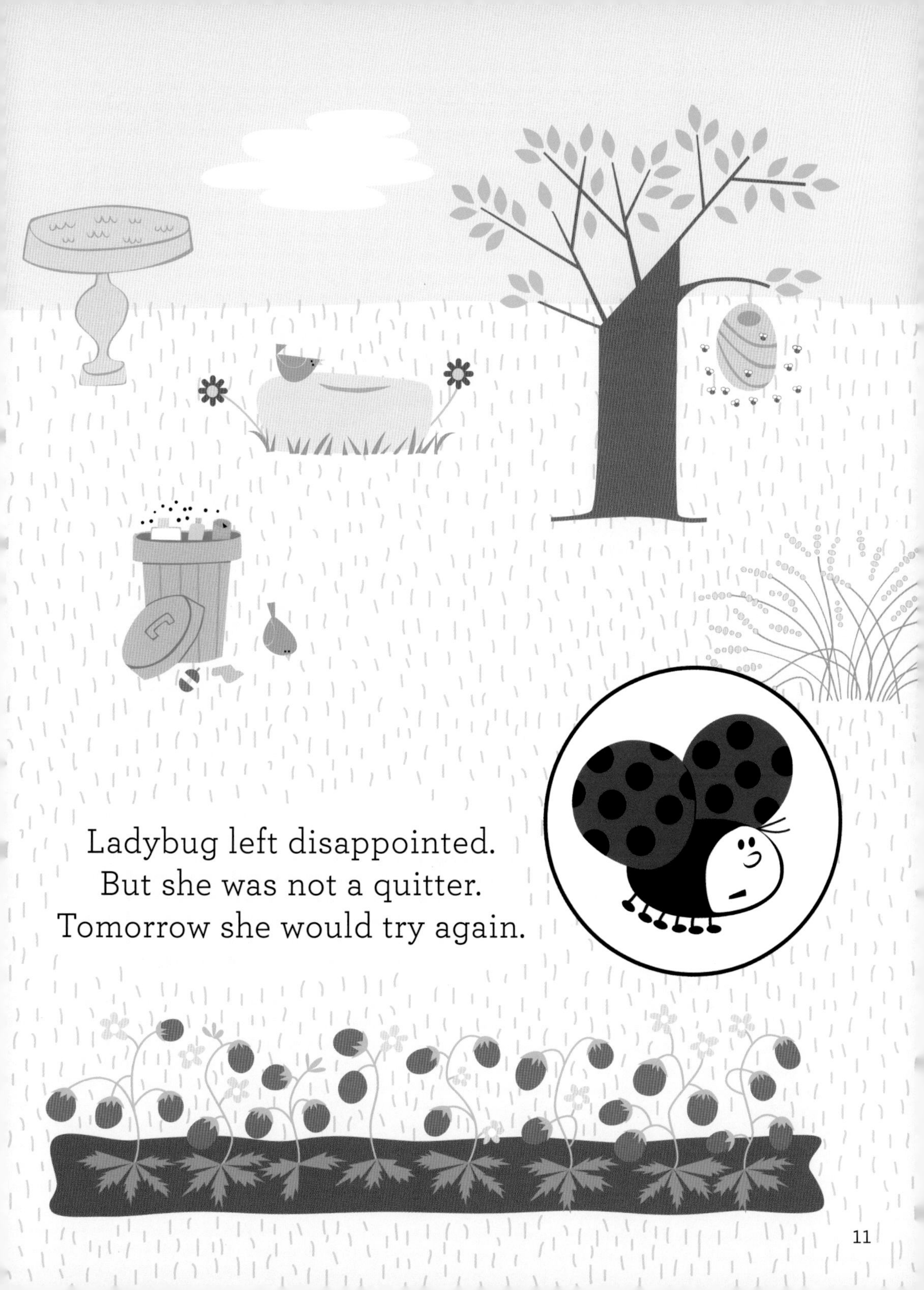

Ladybug left disappointed.
But she was not a quitter.
Tomorrow she would try again.

The next day, as usual, Ladybug was back. And she couldn't believe her eyes. Snail had eaten so many sweet **RED** strawberries, he had turned **GREEN**.

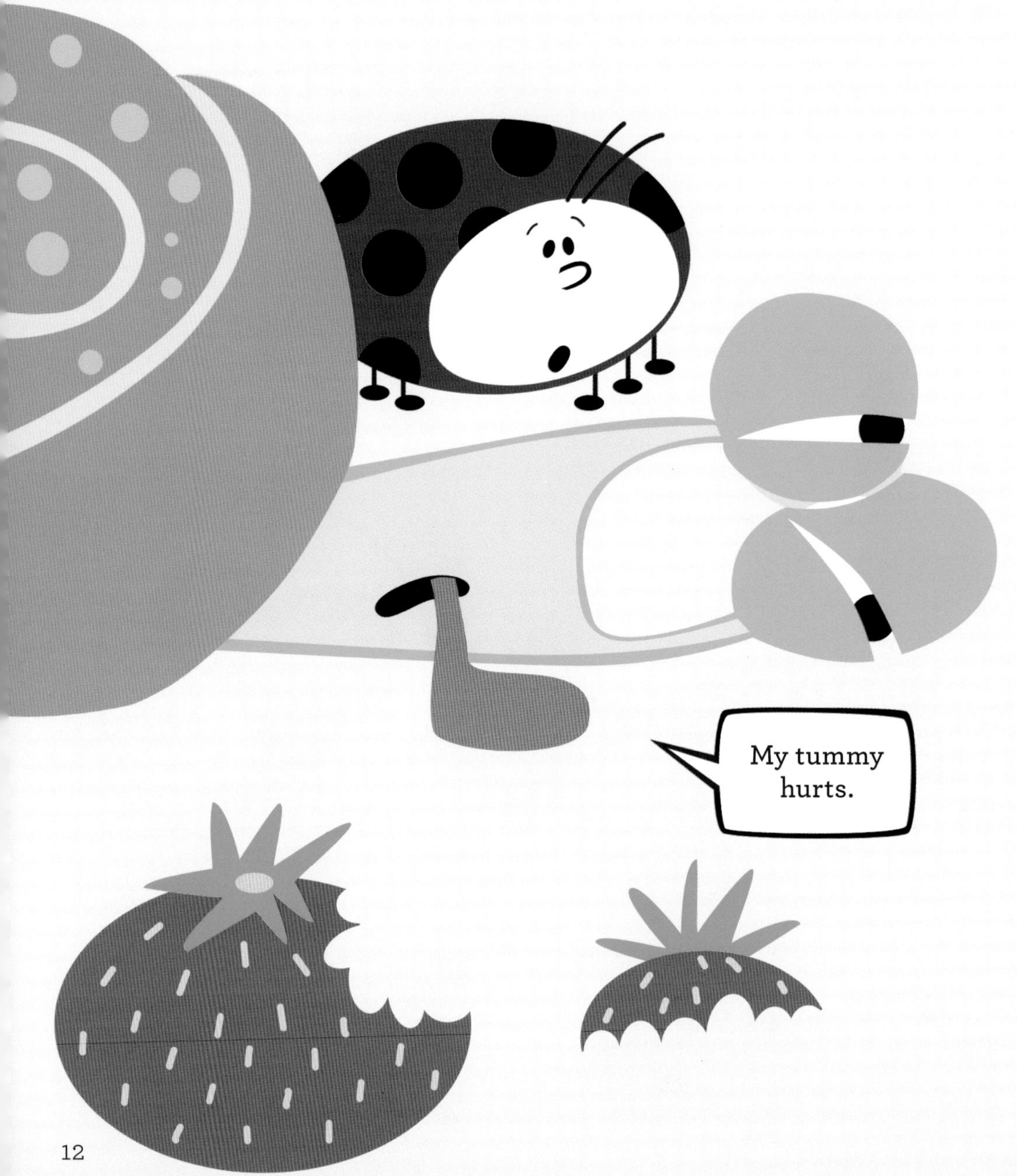
My tummy hurts.

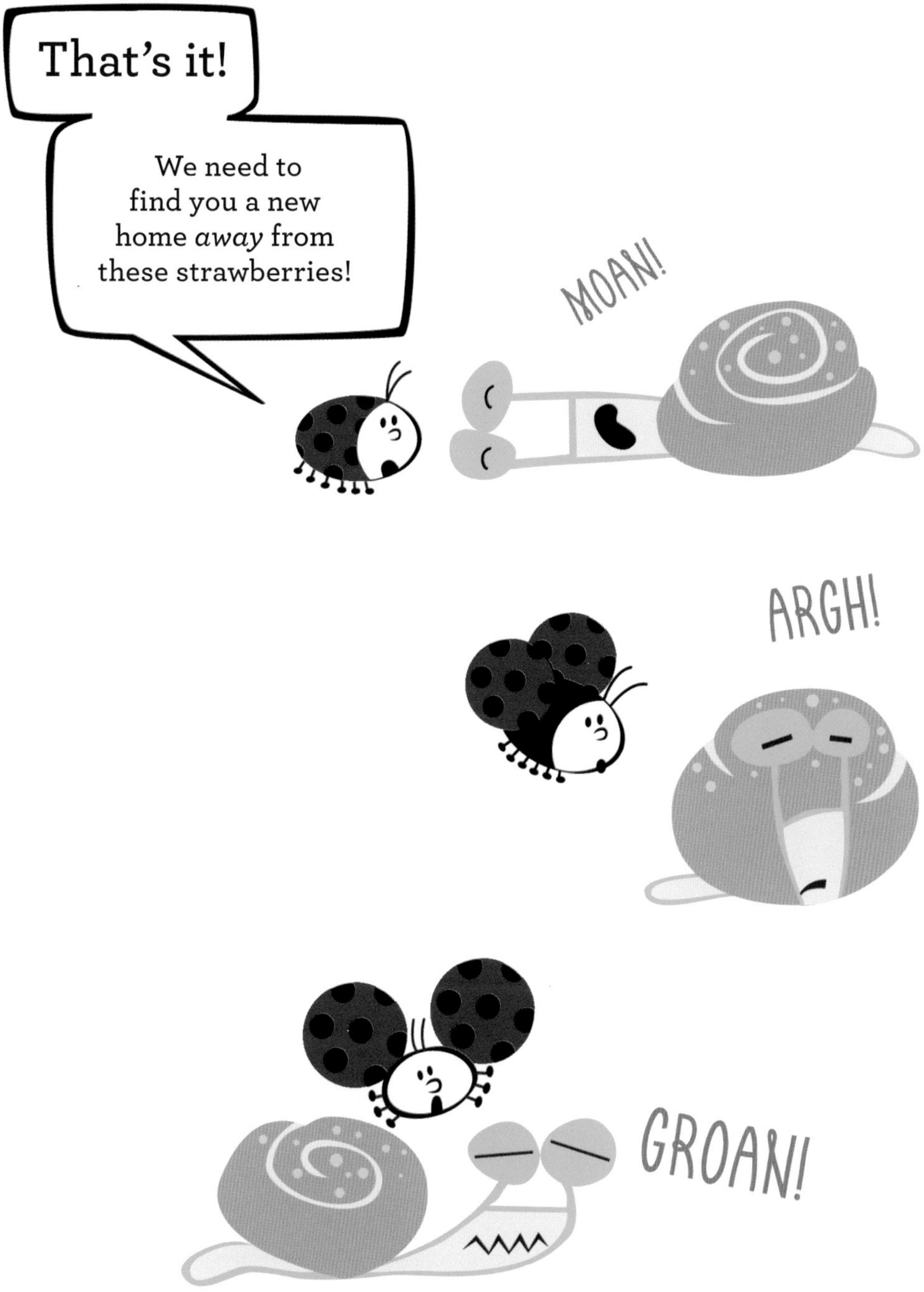
That's it!
We need to find you a new home *away* from these strawberries!
MOAN!
ARGH!
GROAN!

Before Snail could answer . . .

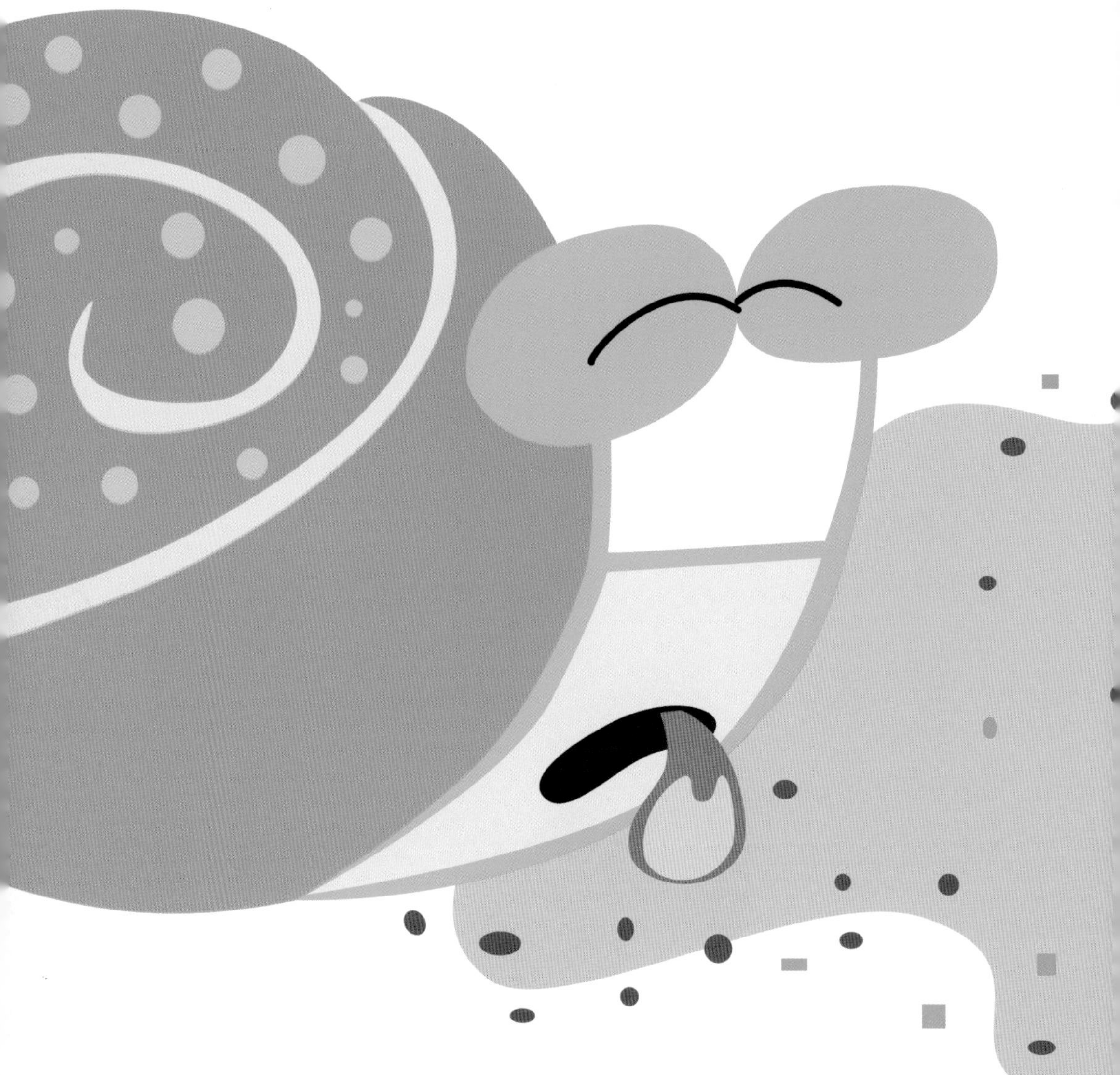

he threw up.

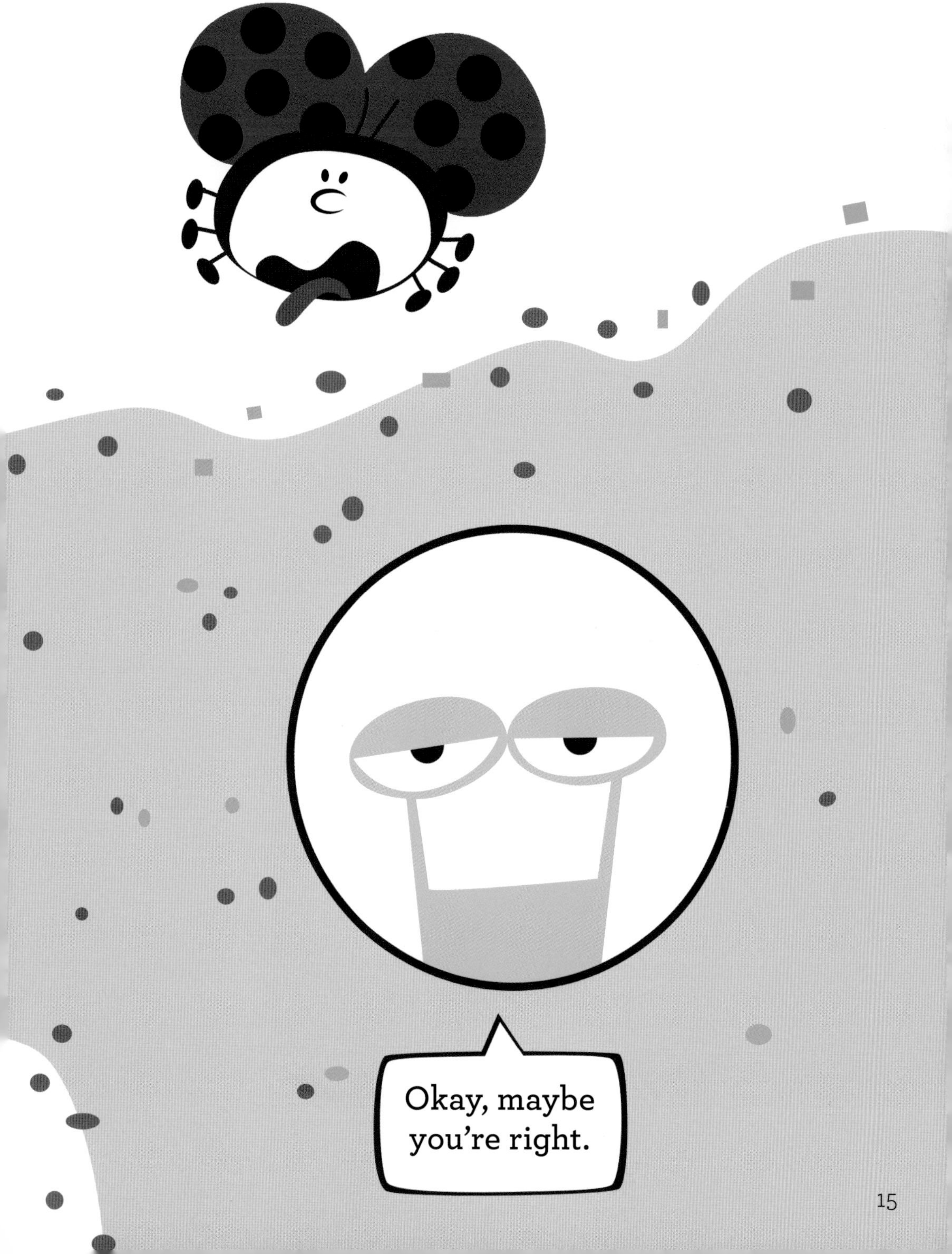
Okay, maybe you’re right.

CHAPTER 2

Early the next morning, Ladybug met Snail
with a long list of places to visit.

honeysuckle
trash can
birdbath
rock
beehive
ambrosia
apple orchard

I'll be your real
estate agent.

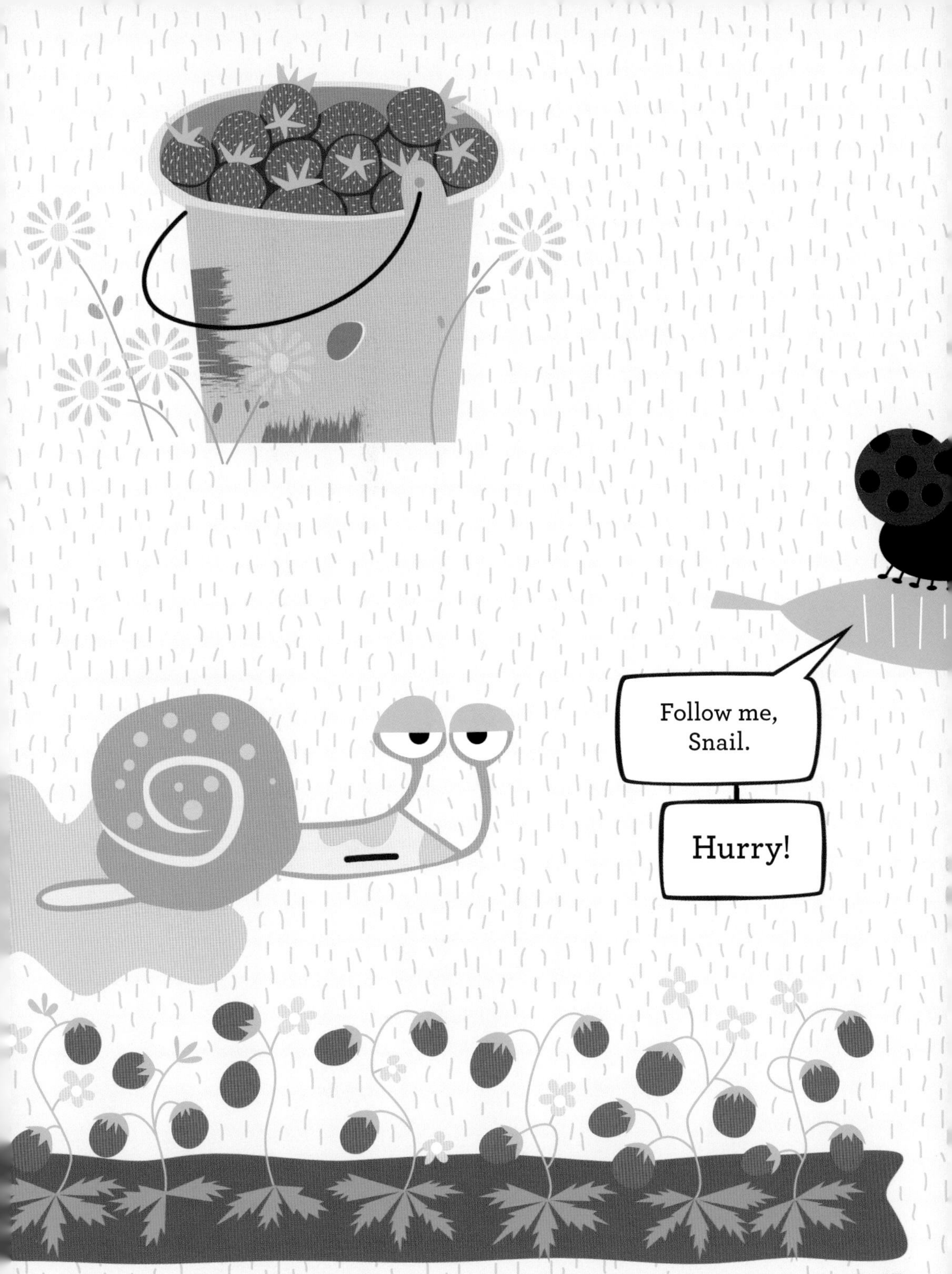
Follow me,
Snail.
Hurry!

Snail followed Ladybug to the top of a fence post.
In the distance, he spied an apple orchard.

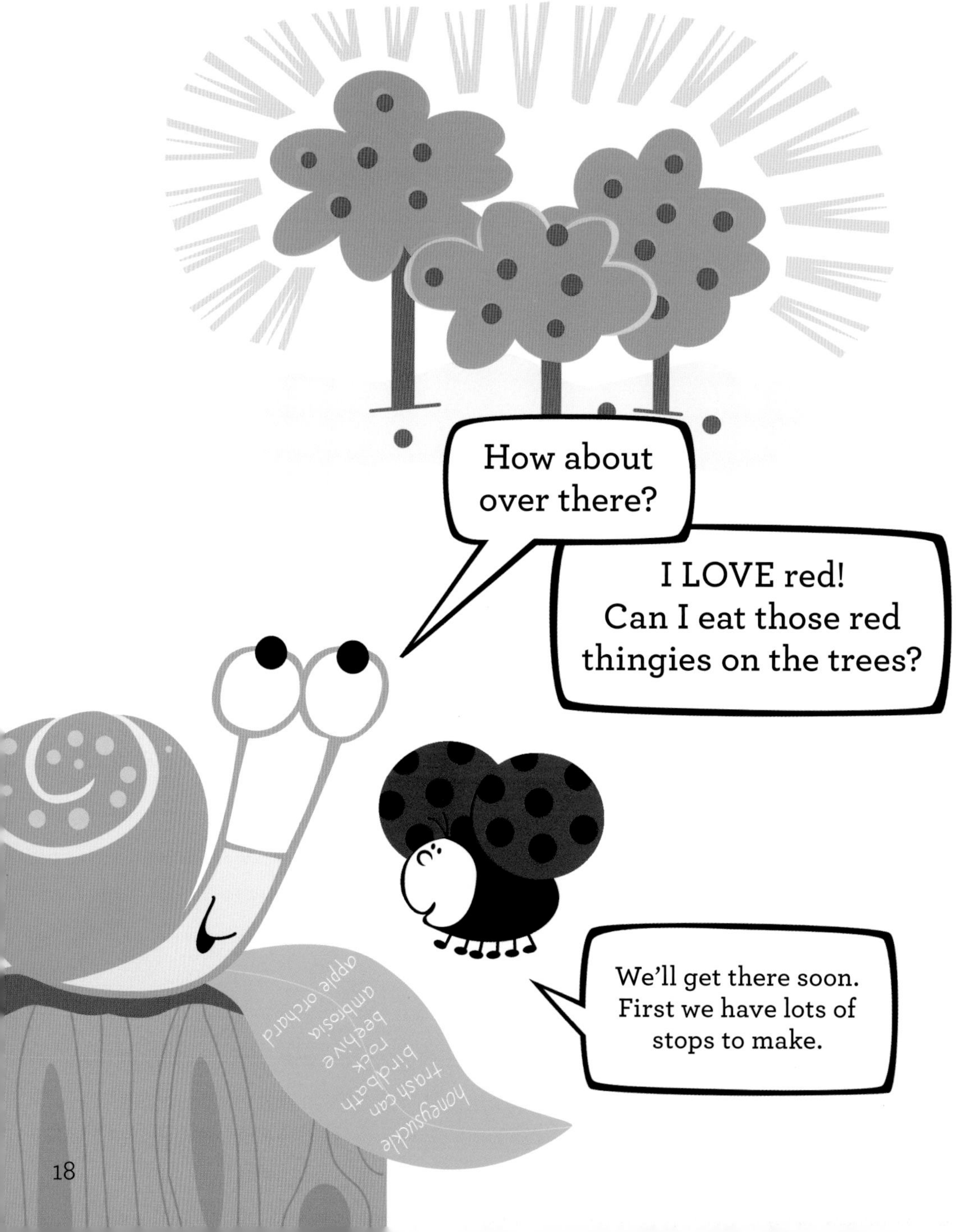
How about over there?
I LOVE red! Can I eat those red thingies on the trees?
We'll get there soon. First we have lots of stops to make.
apple orchard
ambrosia
beehive
rock
birdbath
trash can
honeysuckle

While Ladybug checked her list, Snail slimed down the fence post and . . .

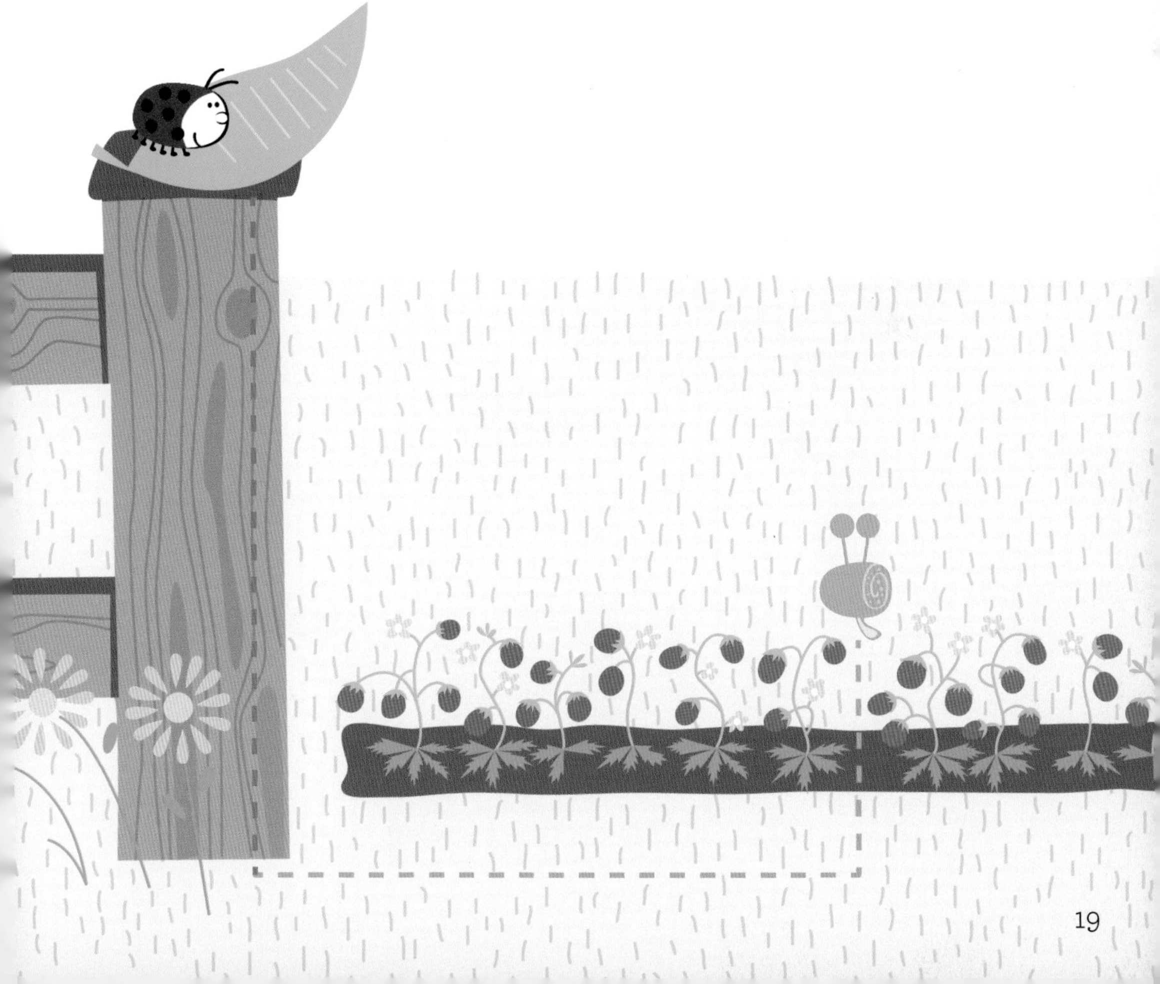

wandered in the direction
of the apple orchard.

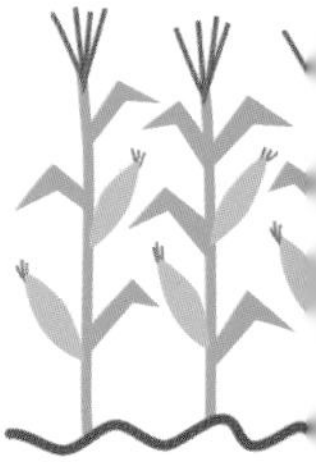

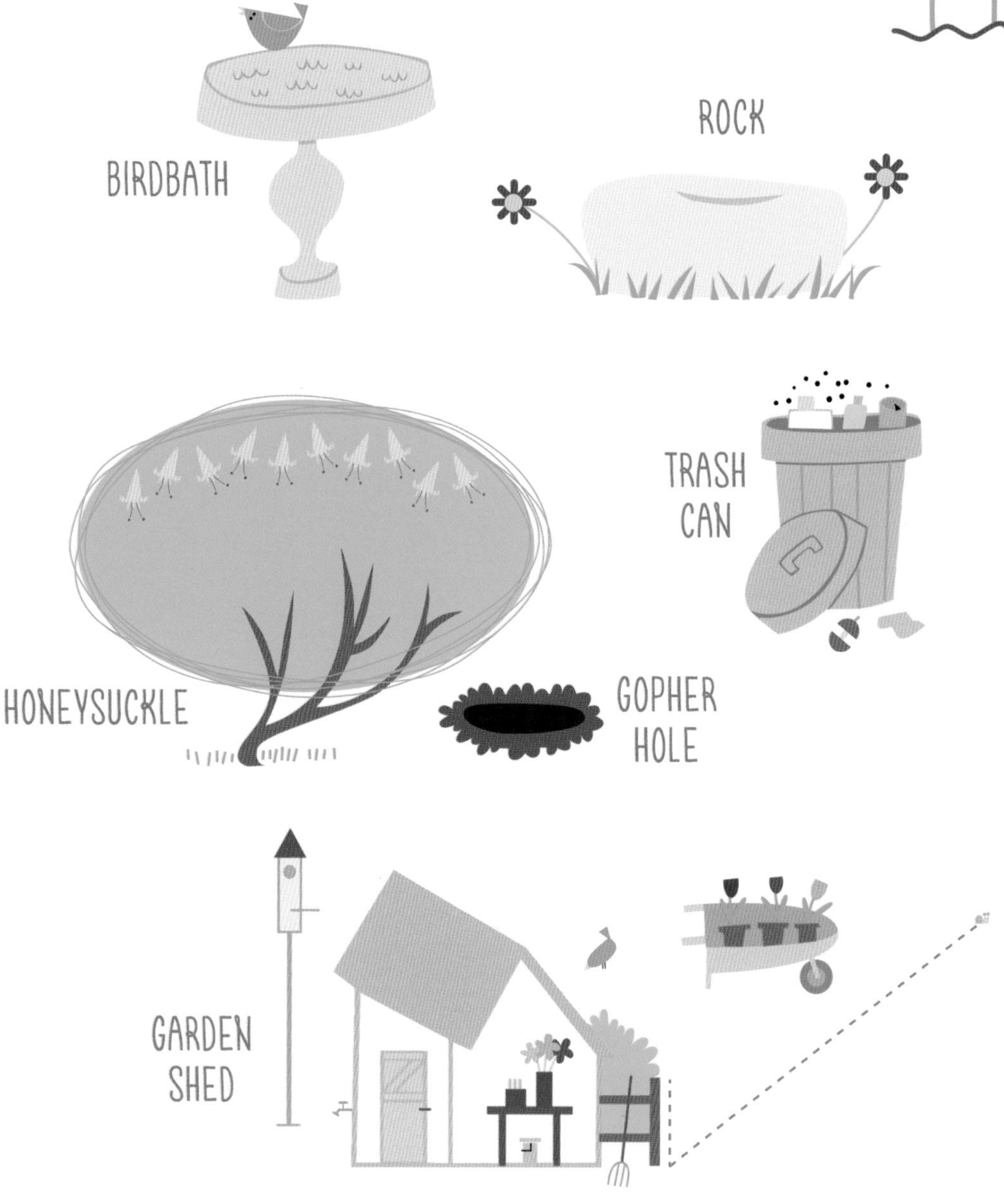
BIRDBATH
ROCK
TRASH CAN
HONEYSUCKLE
GOPHER HOLE
GARDEN SHED

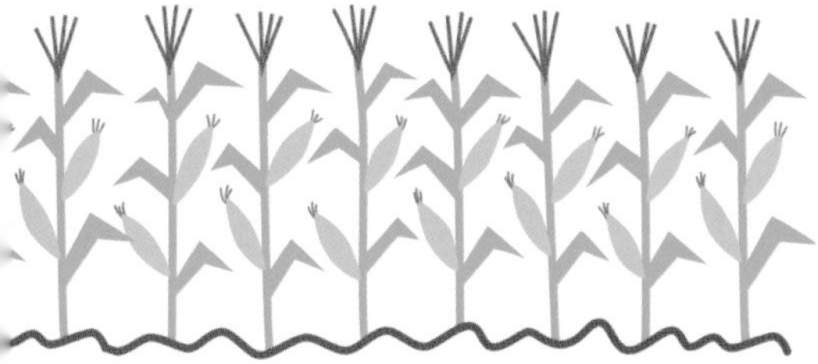

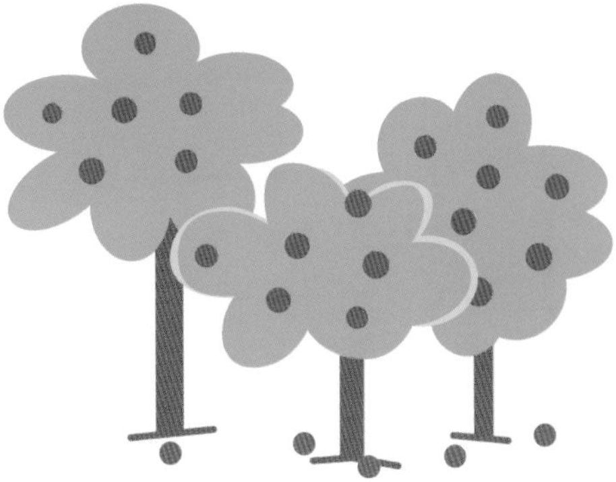

APPLE ORCHARD

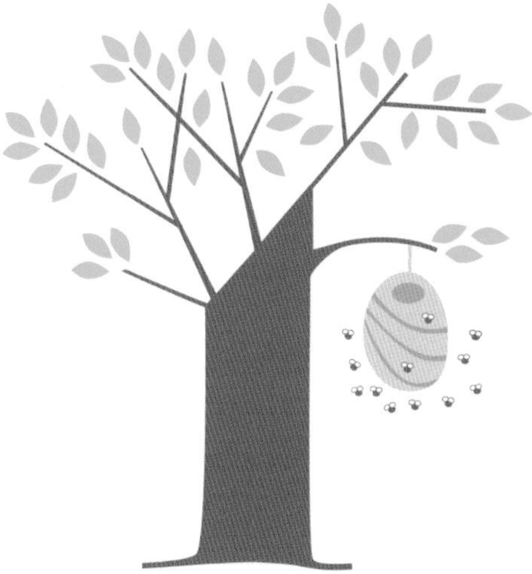

BEEHIVE

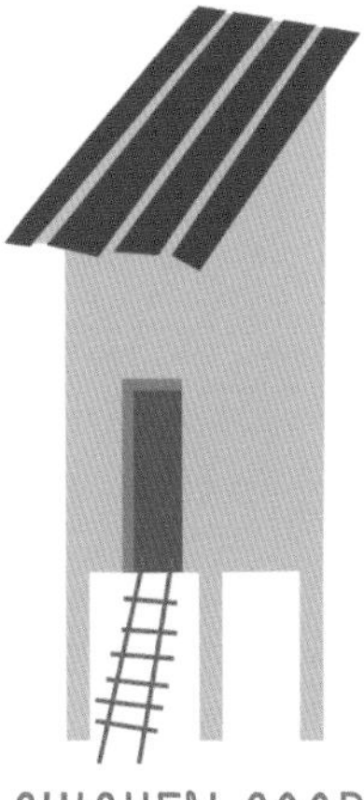

CHICKEN COOP

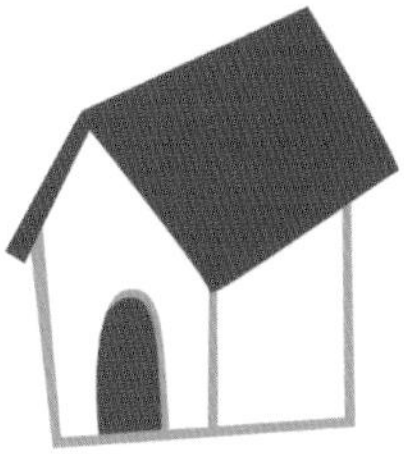

DOGHOUSE

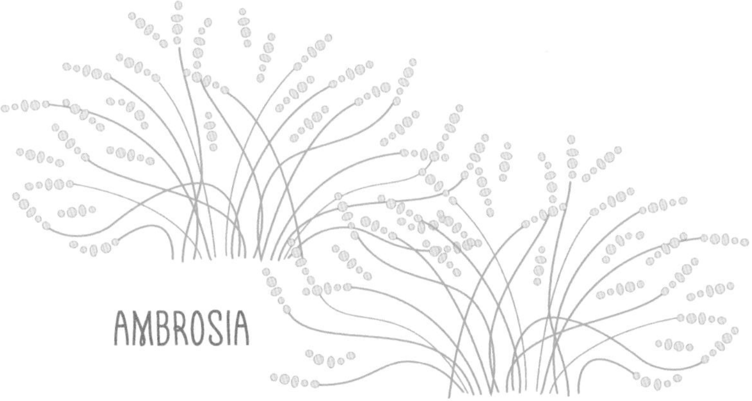

AMBROSIA

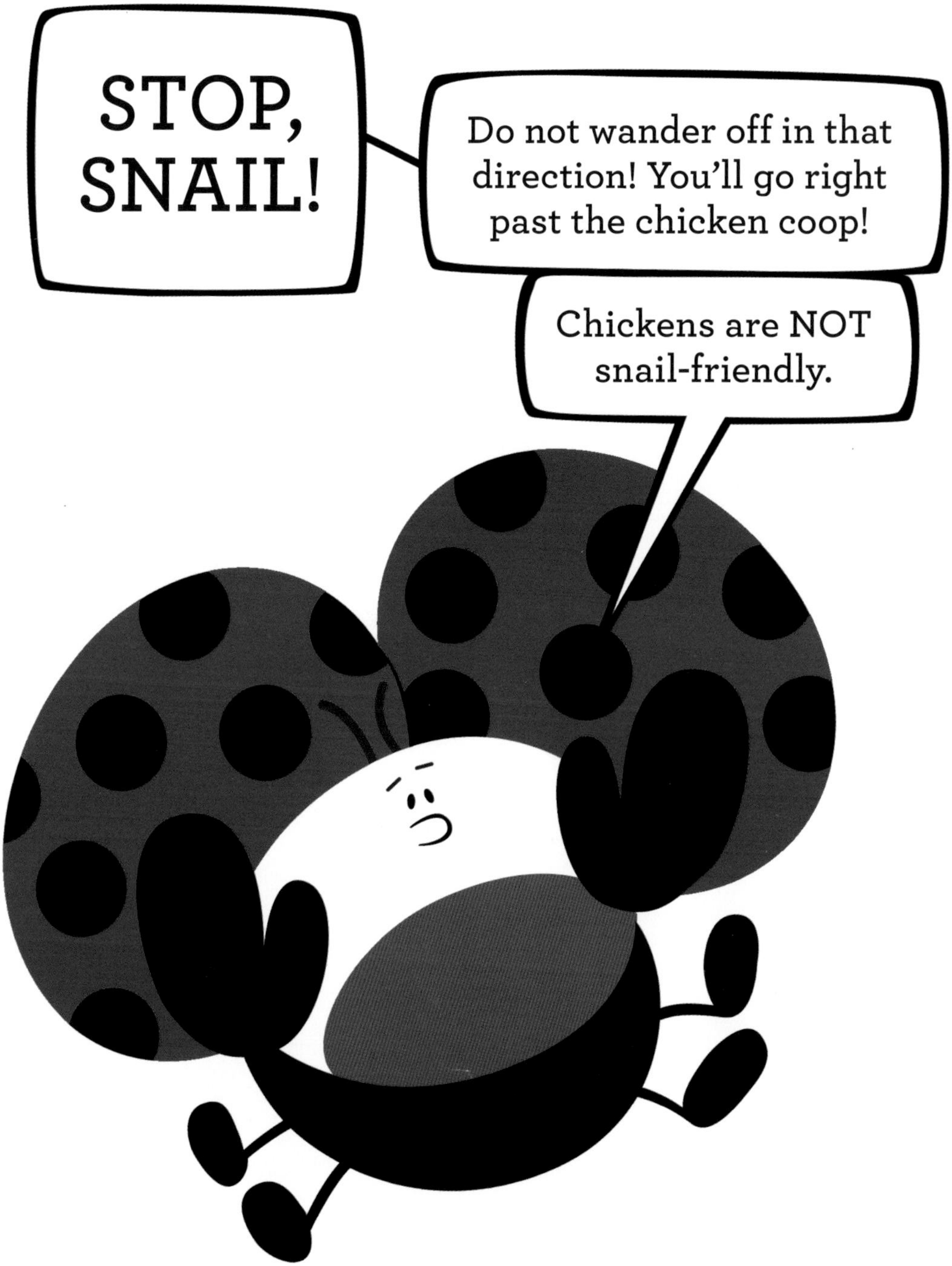
STOP, SNAIL!
Do not wander off in that direction! You'll go right past the chicken coop!
Chickens are NOT snail-friendly.

Now, if Snail had ever seen a chicken or a chicken coop, he would have known this was excellent advice. But he hadn't, so he didn't.

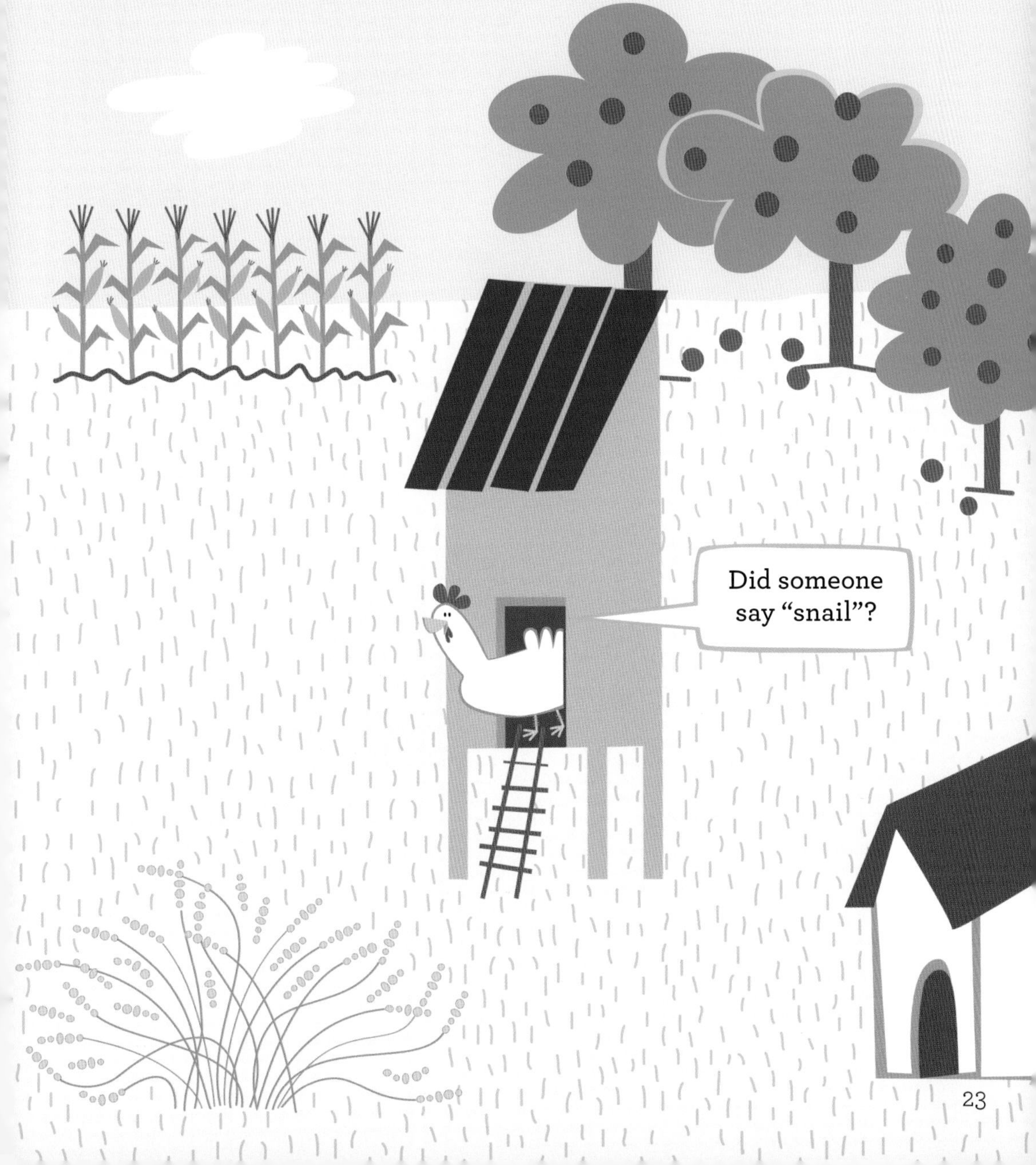
Did someone say "snail"?

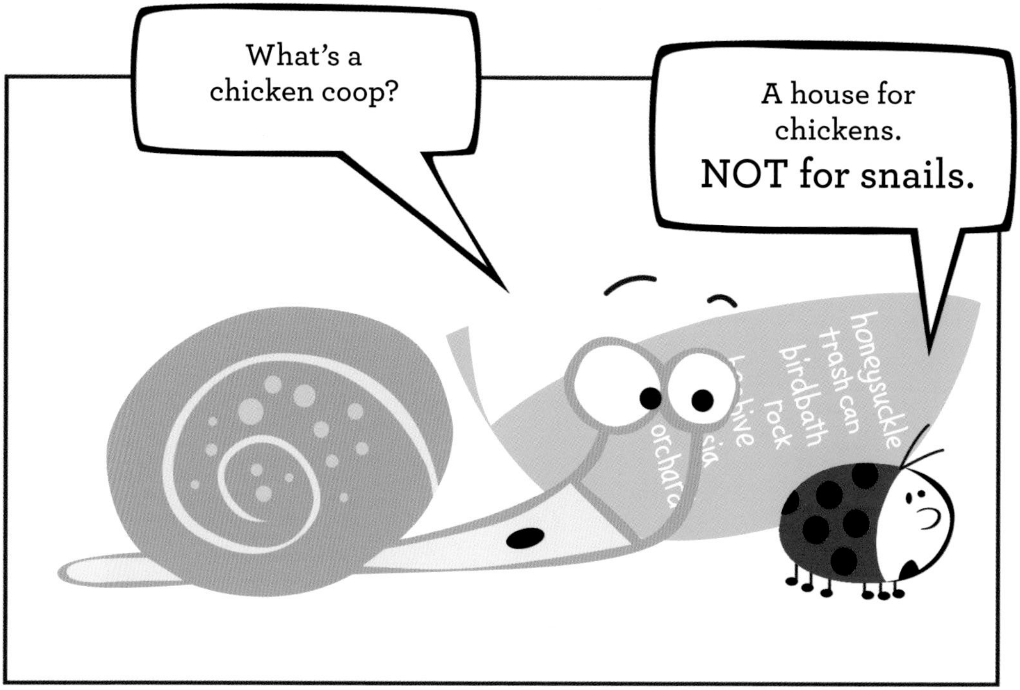
What's a chicken coop?
A house for chickens. NOT for snails.
honeysuckle
trash can
birdbath
rock
orchard

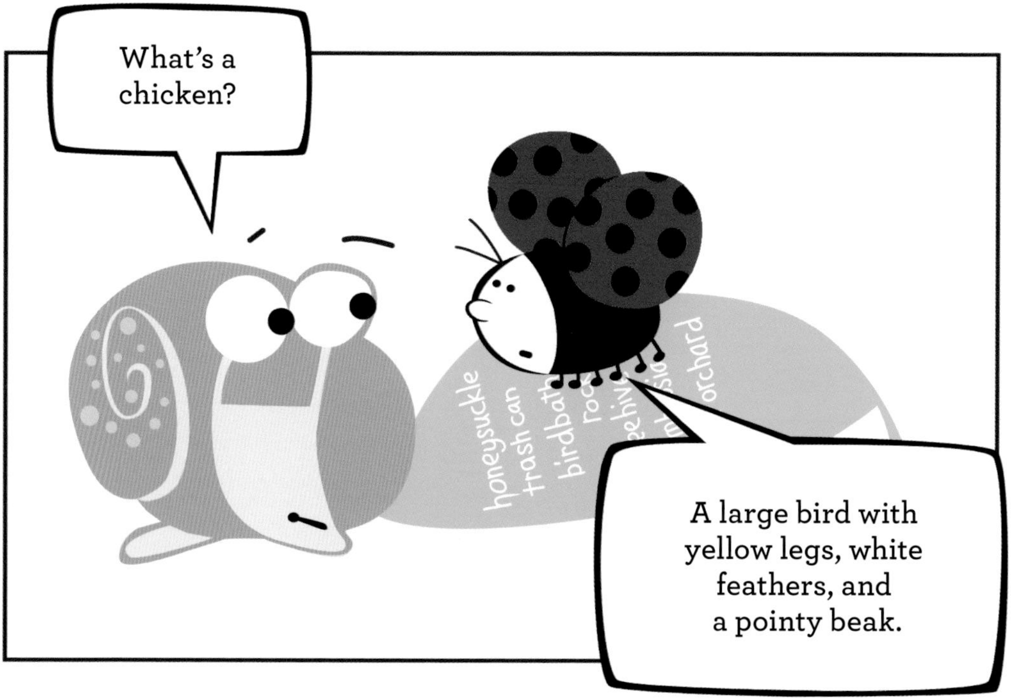
What's a chicken?
A large bird with yellow legs, white feathers, and a pointy beak.
honeysuckle
trash can
orchard

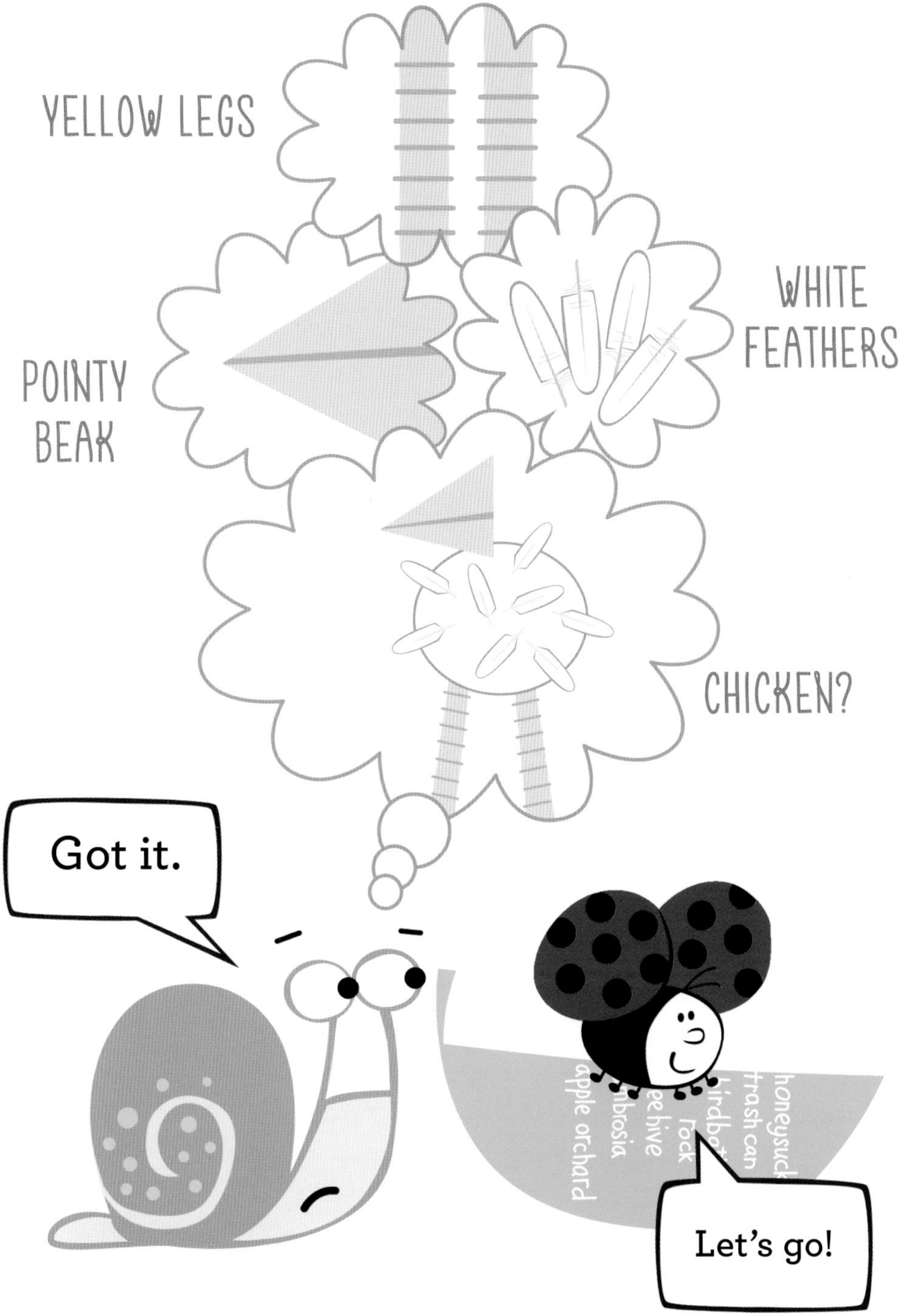
YELLOW LEGS
POINTY BEAK
WHITE FEATHERS
CHICKEN?
Got it.
apple orchard
rock
trash can
Let's go!

CHAPTER 3

Ladybug led Snail to her favorite honeysuckle bush.

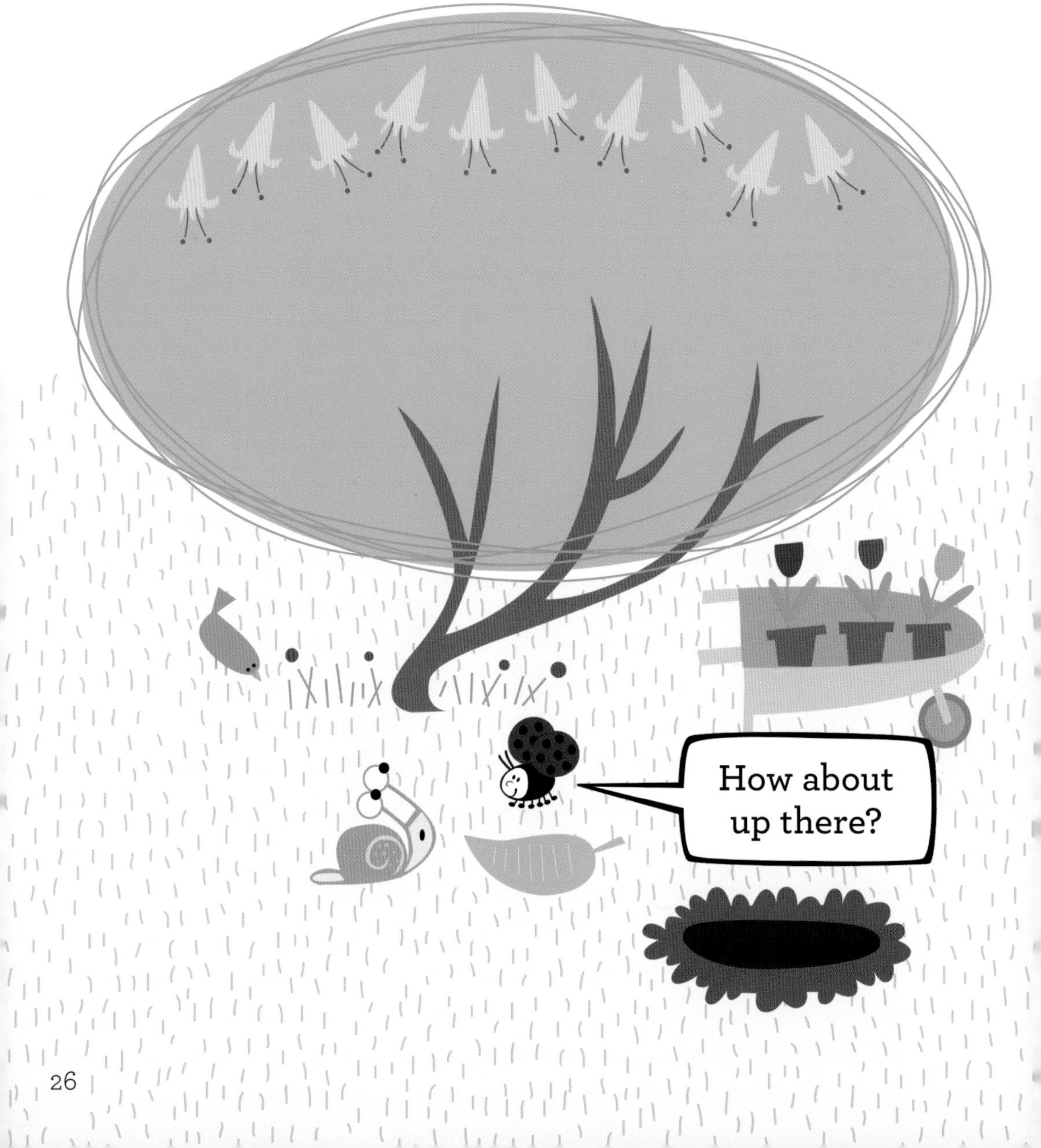
How about up there?

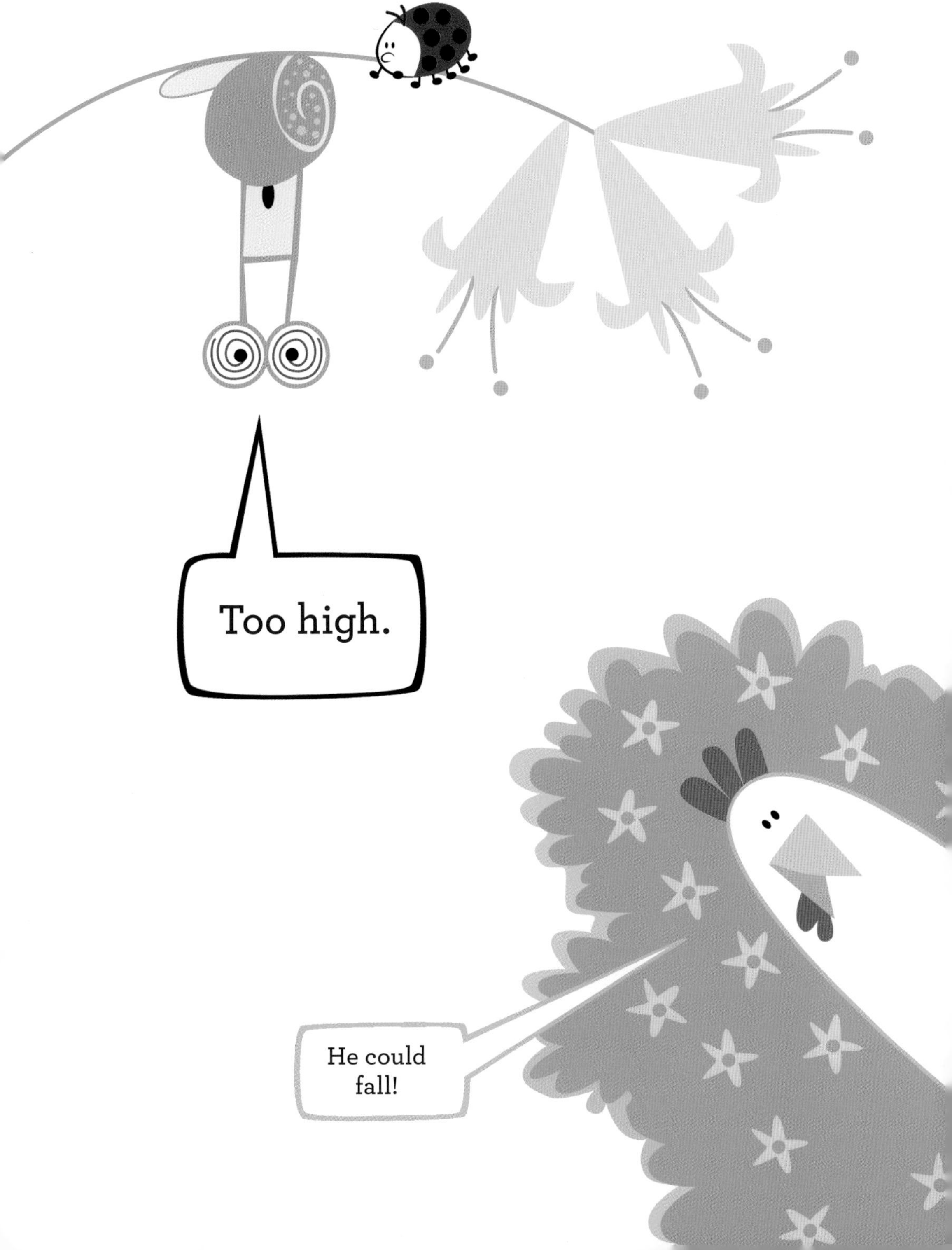
Too high.
He could fall!

Just then, Snail and Ladybug
heard a familiar voice.

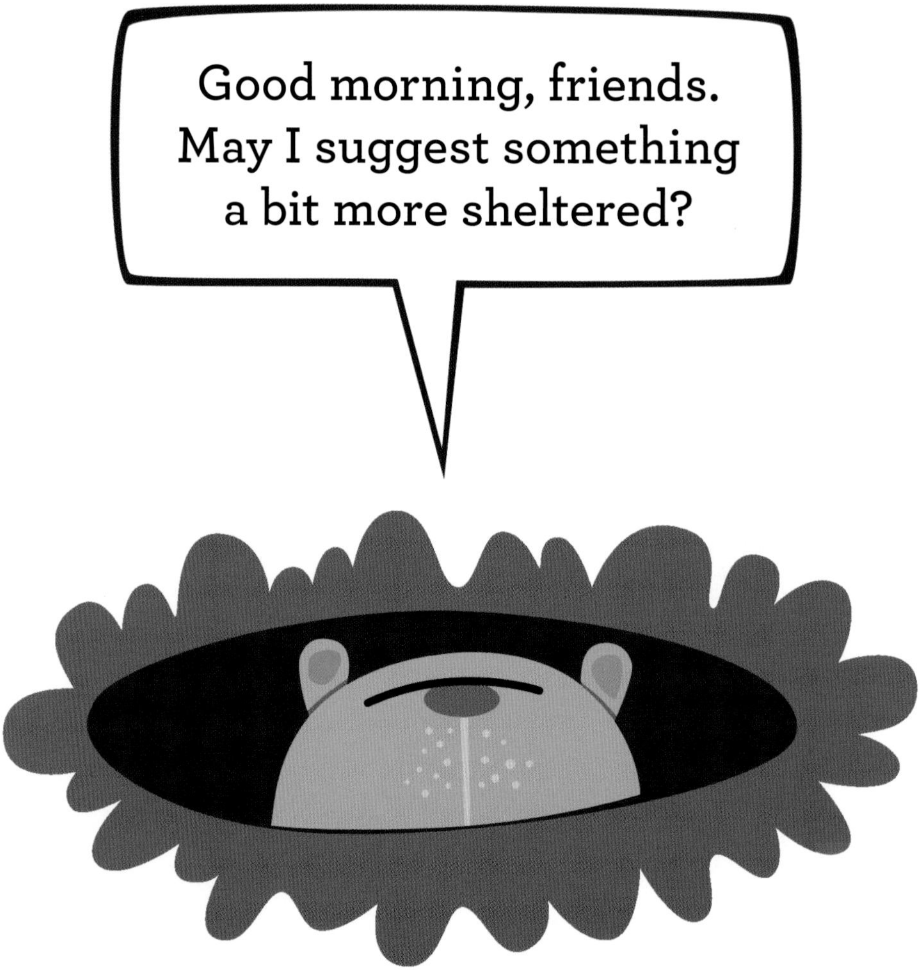
Good morning, friends. May I suggest something a bit more sheltered?

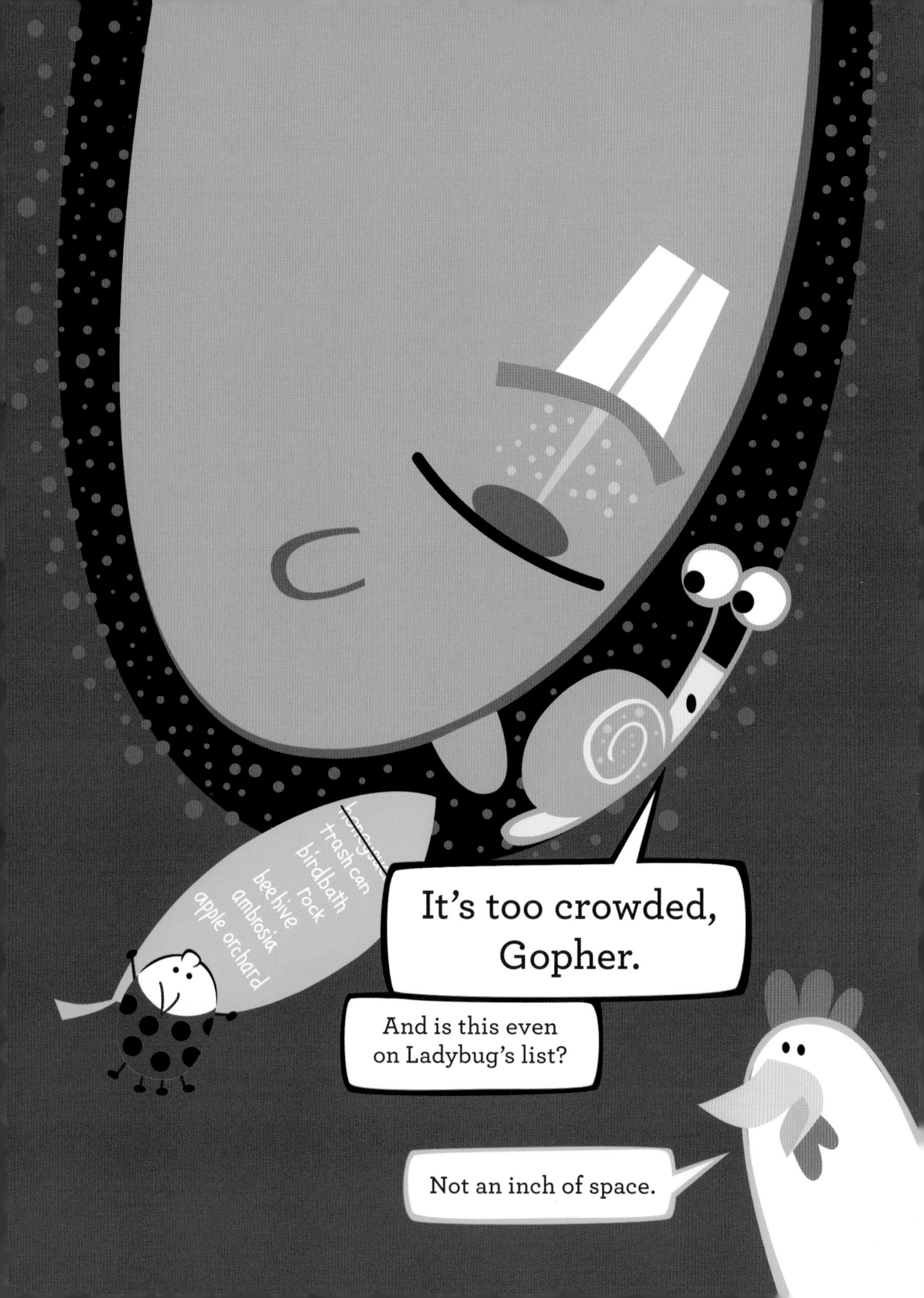
trash can
birdbath
rock
beehive
ambrosia
apple orchard
It's too crowded, Gopher.
And is this even on Ladybug's list?
Not an inch of space.

Ladybug continued to show Snail
the different spots on her list.
Snail continued to find problems with each one.

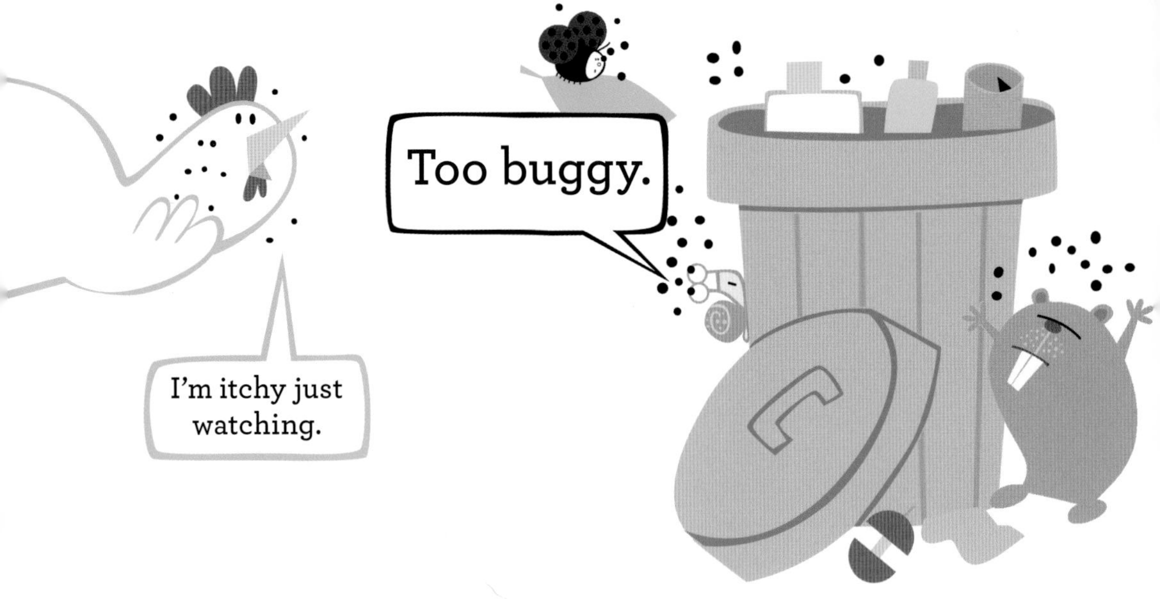
Too buggy.
I'm itchy just watching.

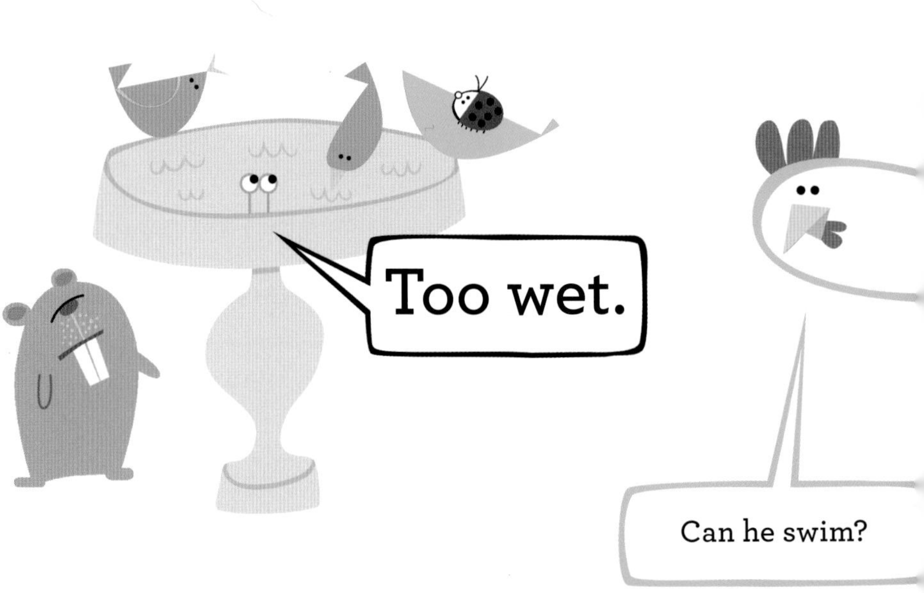
Too wet.
Can he swim?

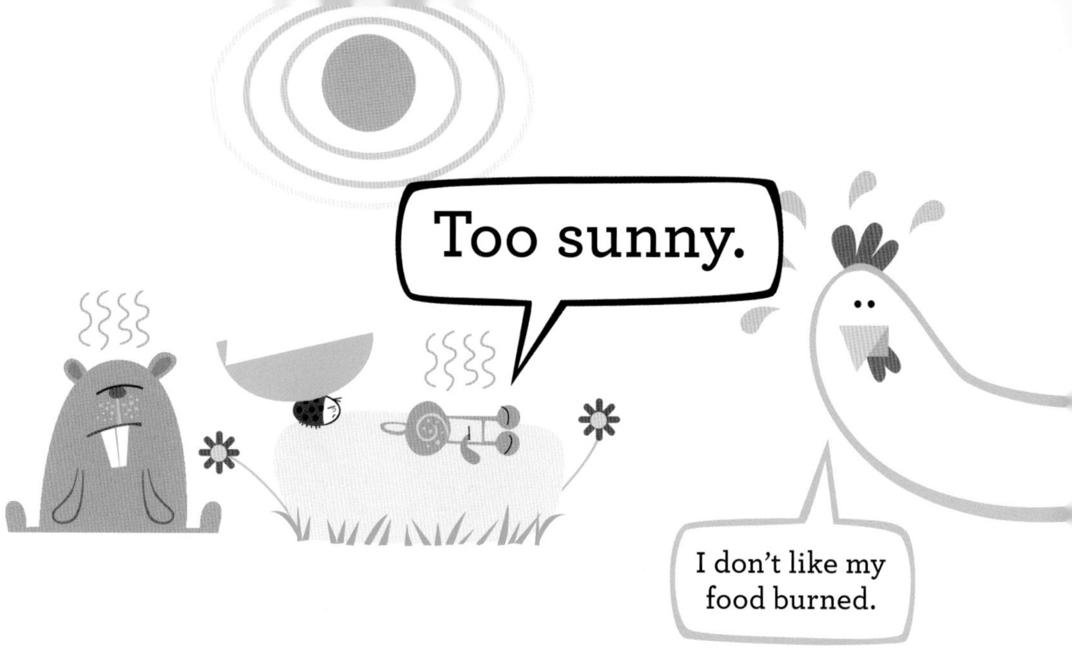

Too sunny.
I don't like my food burned.

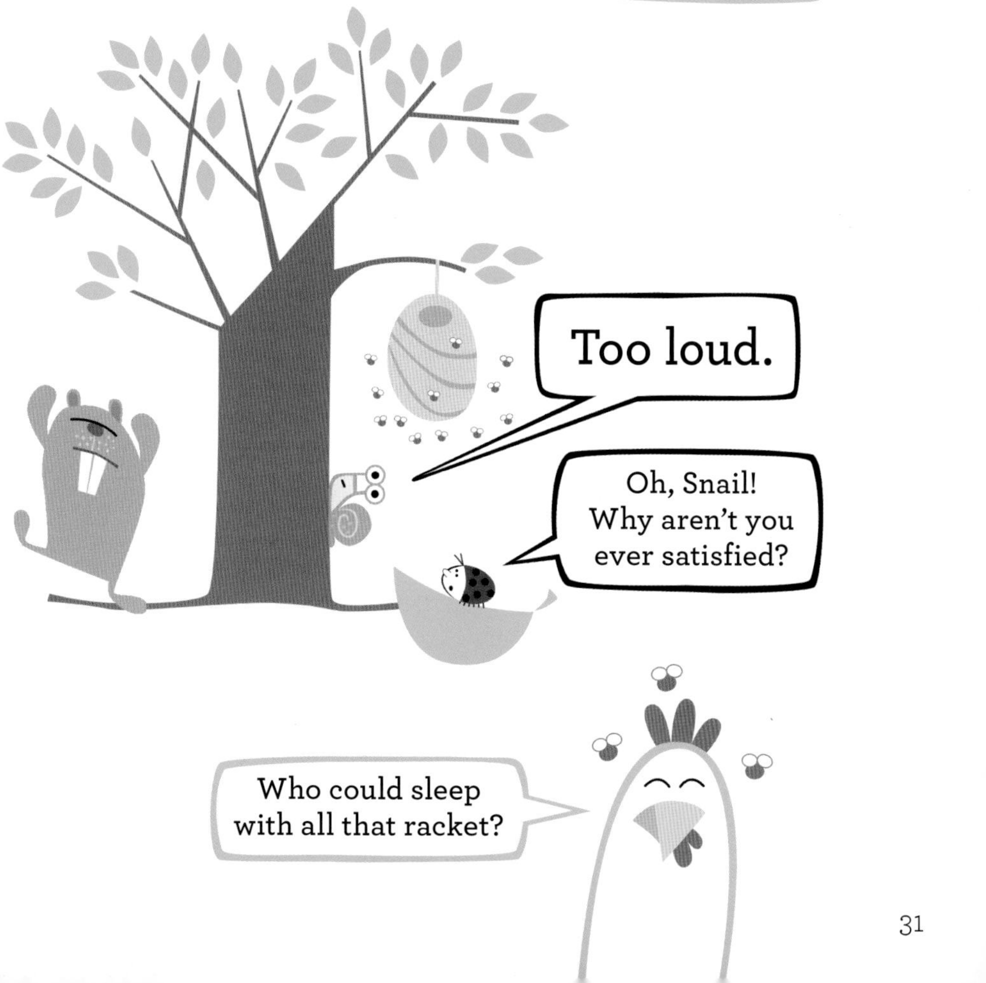

Too loud.
Oh, Snail! Why aren't you ever satisfied?
Who could sleep with all that racket?

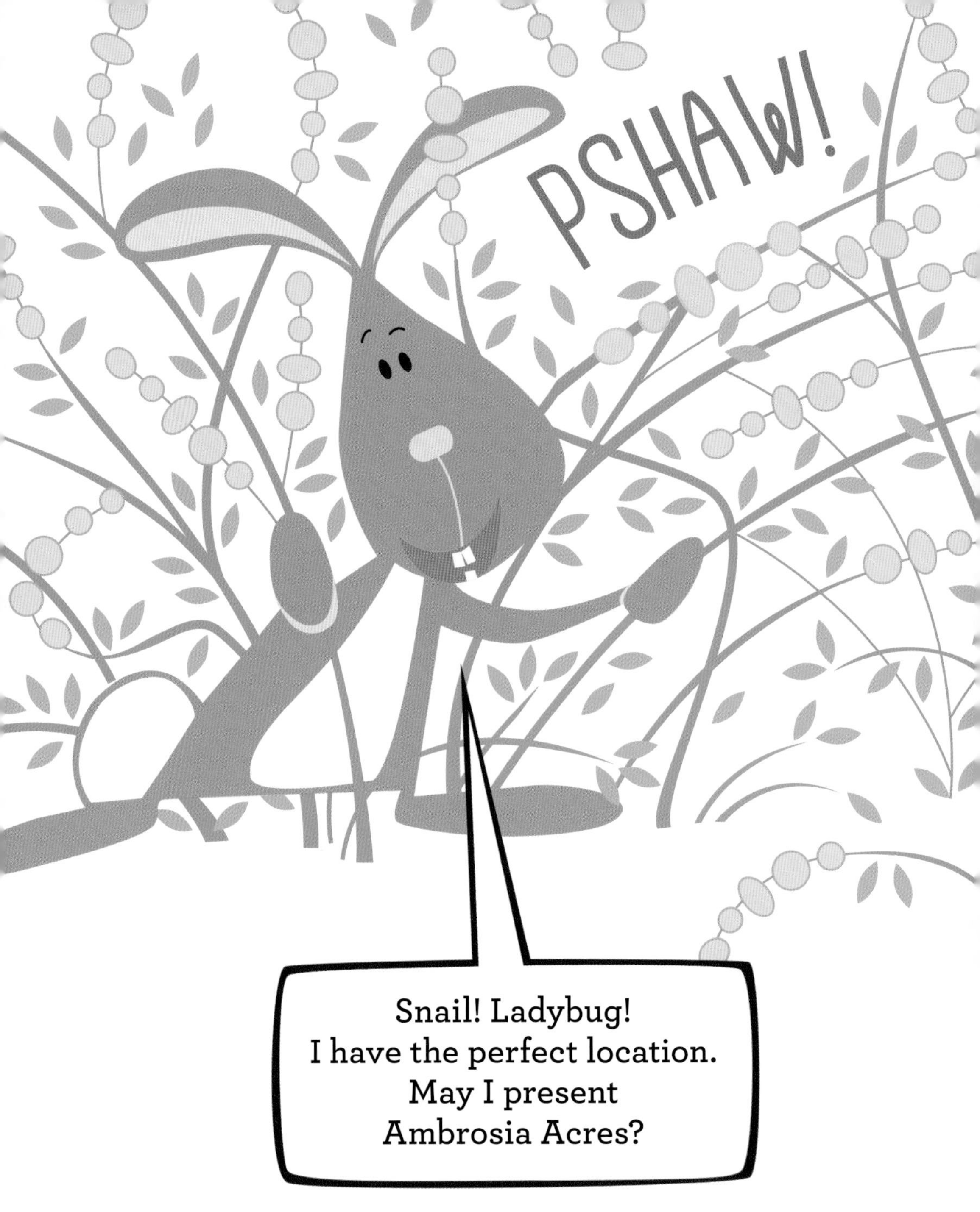
PSHAW!
Snail! Ladybug!
I have the perfect location.
May I present
Ambrosia Acres?

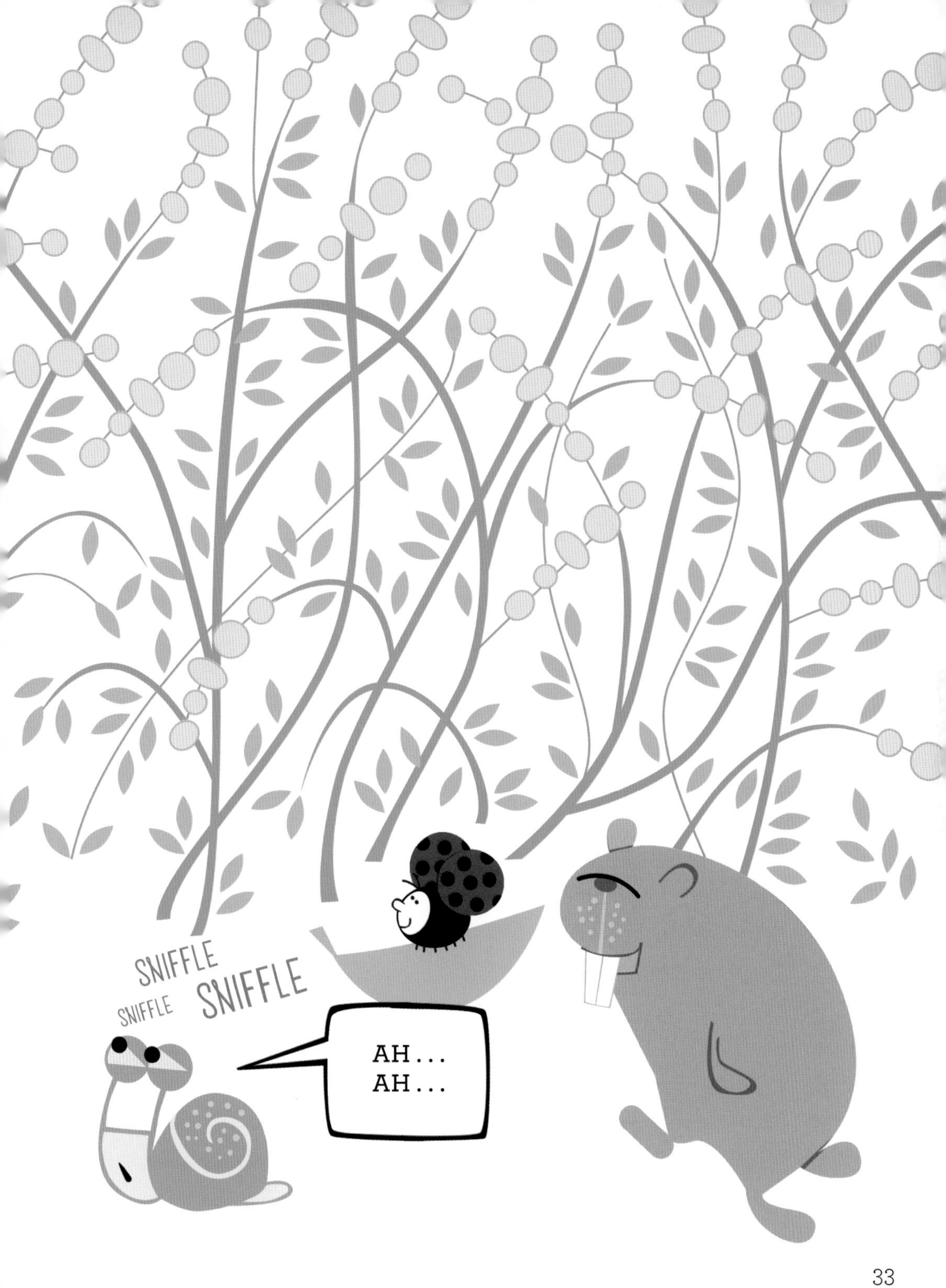
SNIFFLE
SNIFFLE
SNIFFLE
AH...
AH...

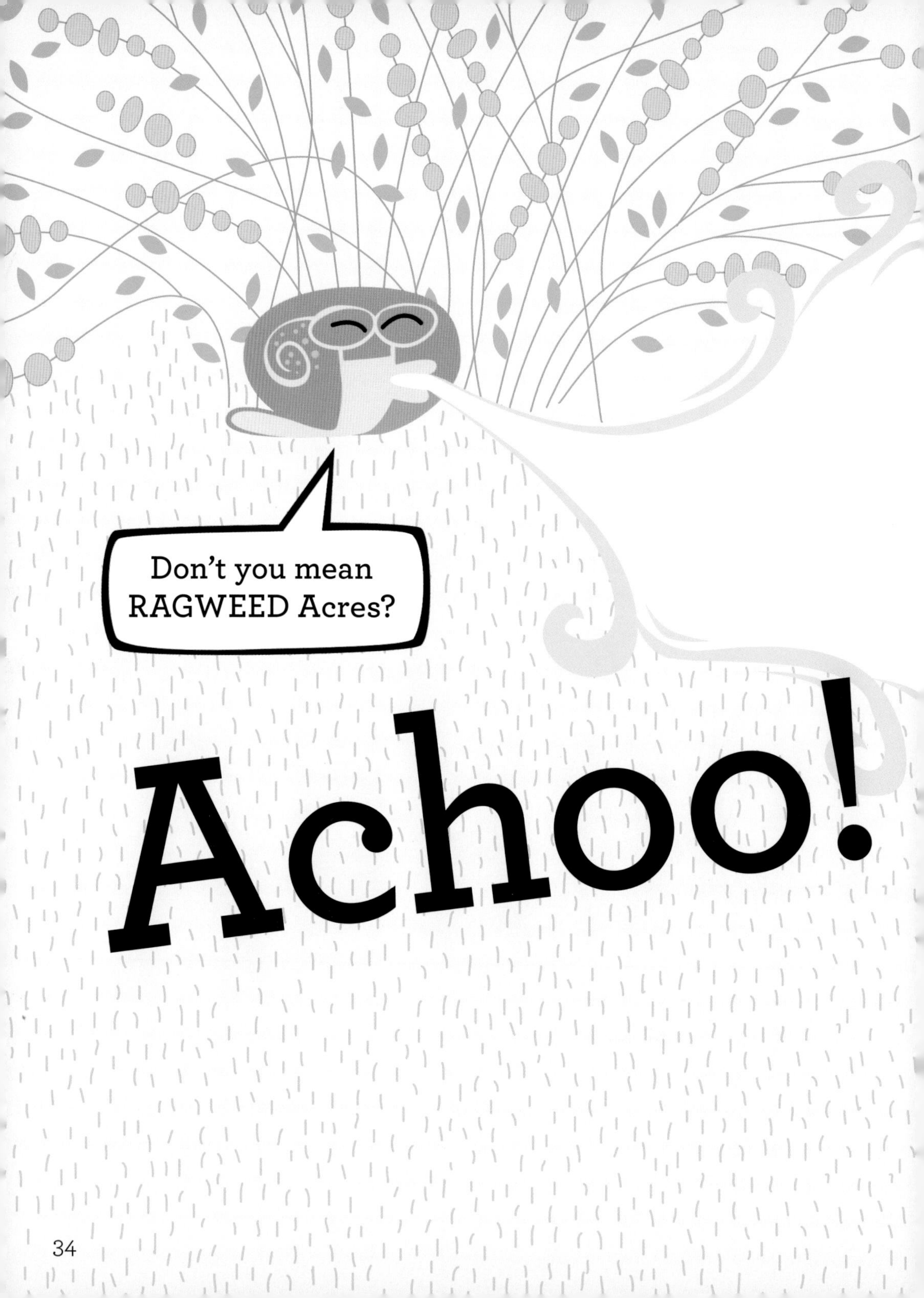
Don't you mean RAGWEED Acres?
Achoo!

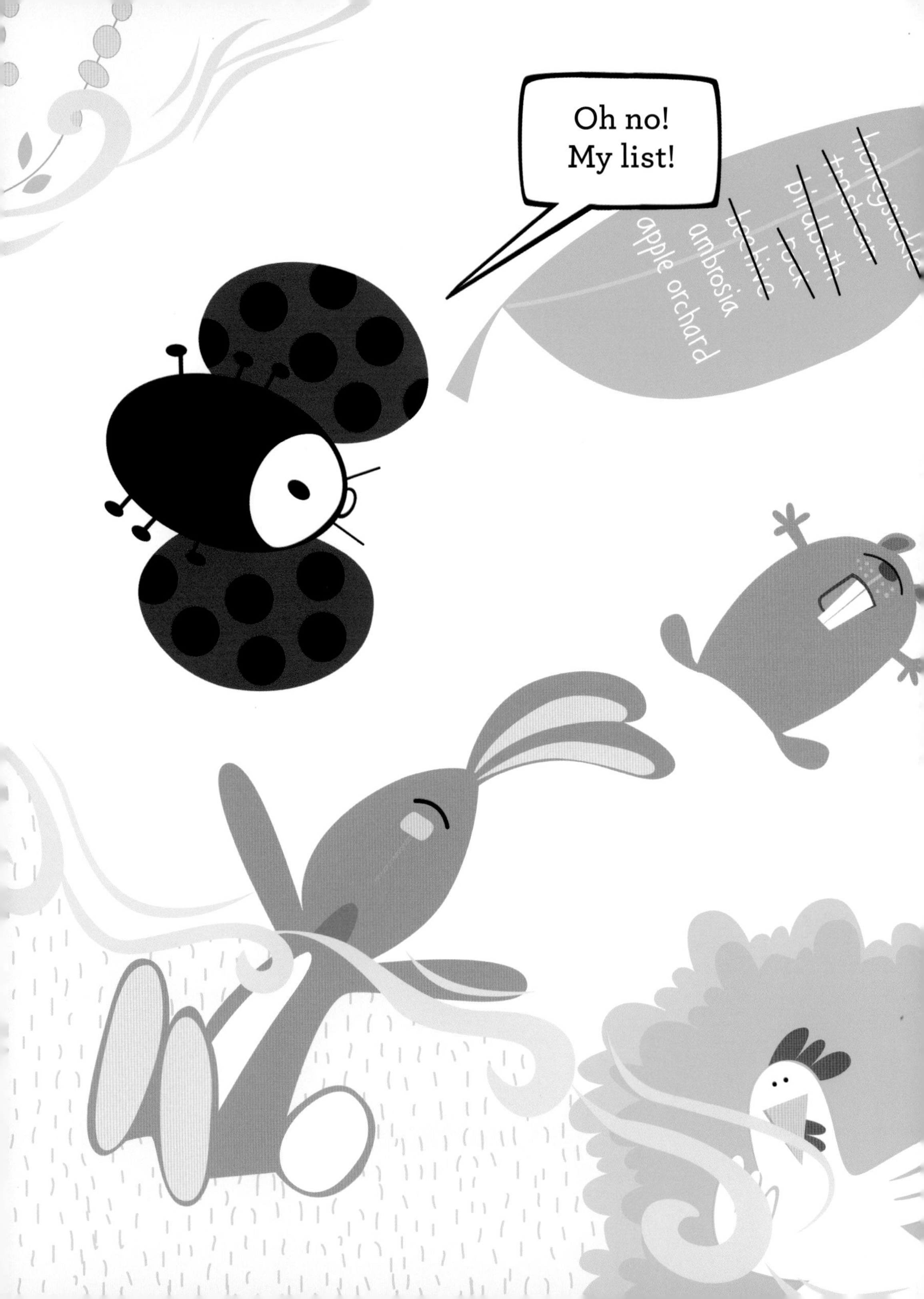
Oh no!
My list!
~~honeysuckle~~
~~trashcan~~
~~birdbath~~
~~rock~~
~~beehive~~
ambrosia
apple orchard

While Ladybug, Gopher, and Rabbit looked for Ladybug's lost list, pretty red thingies once again caught Snail's eye.

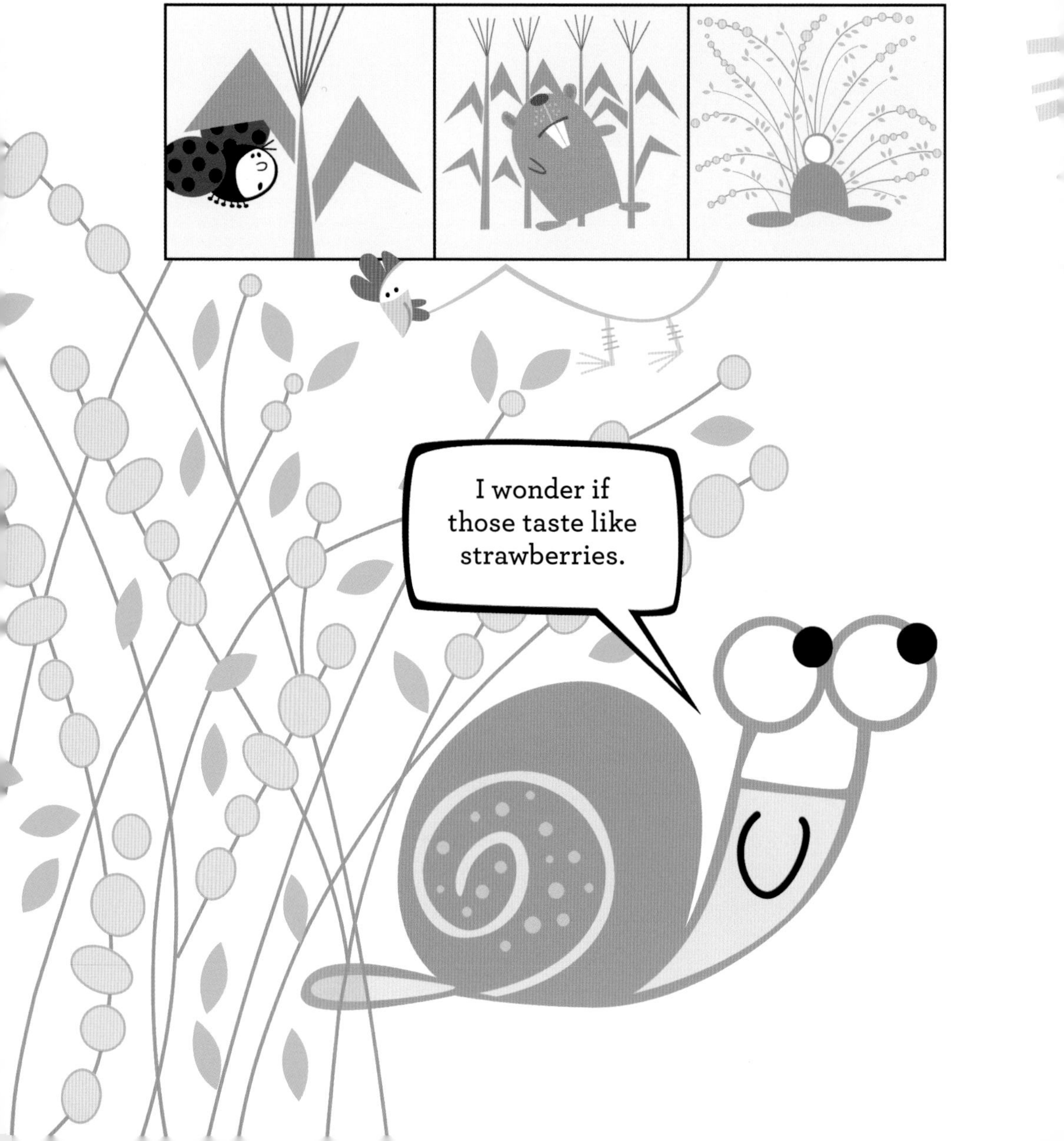
I wonder if those taste like strawberries.

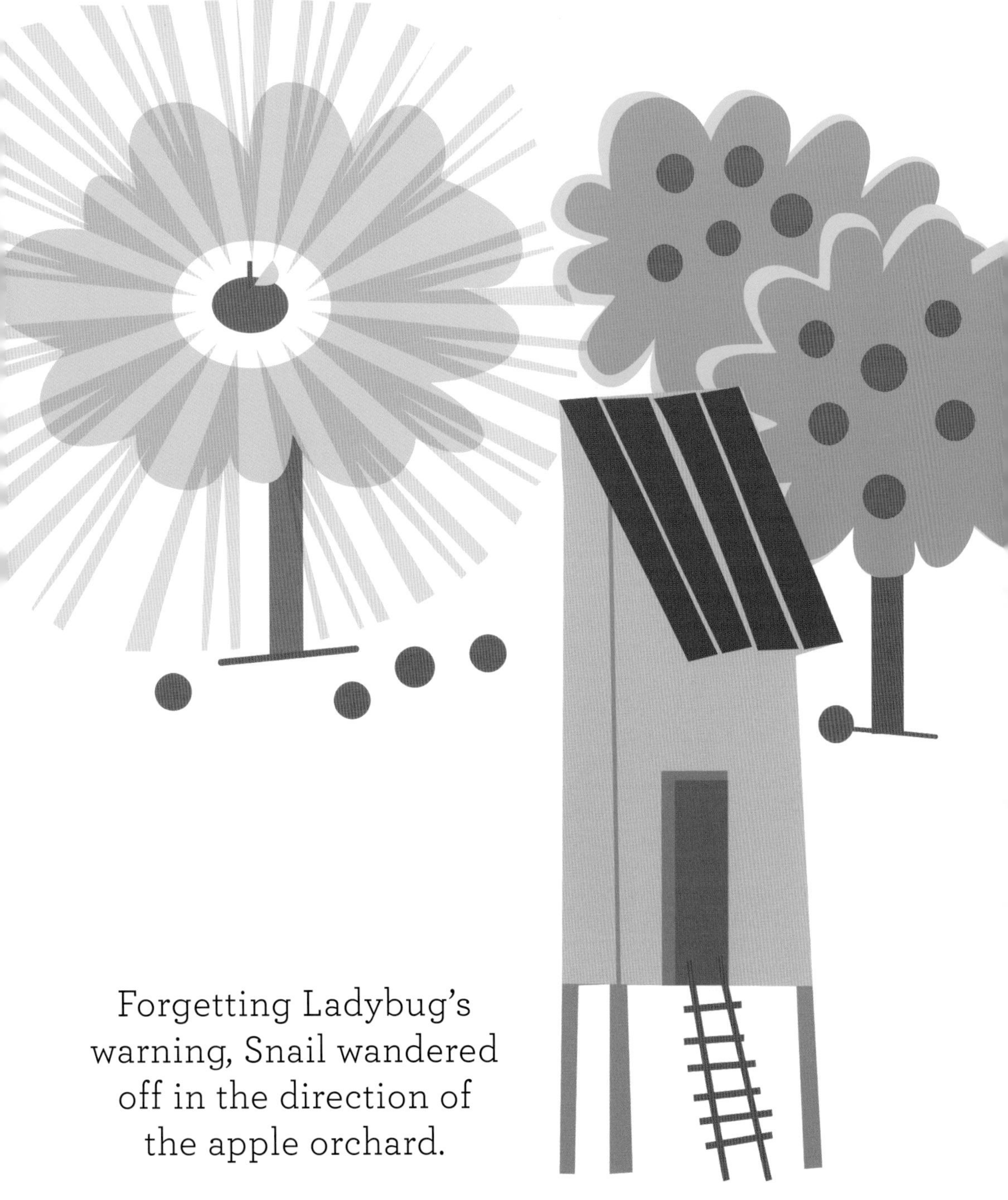

Forgetting Ladybug's
warning, Snail wandered
off in the direction of
the apple orchard.

CHAPTER 4

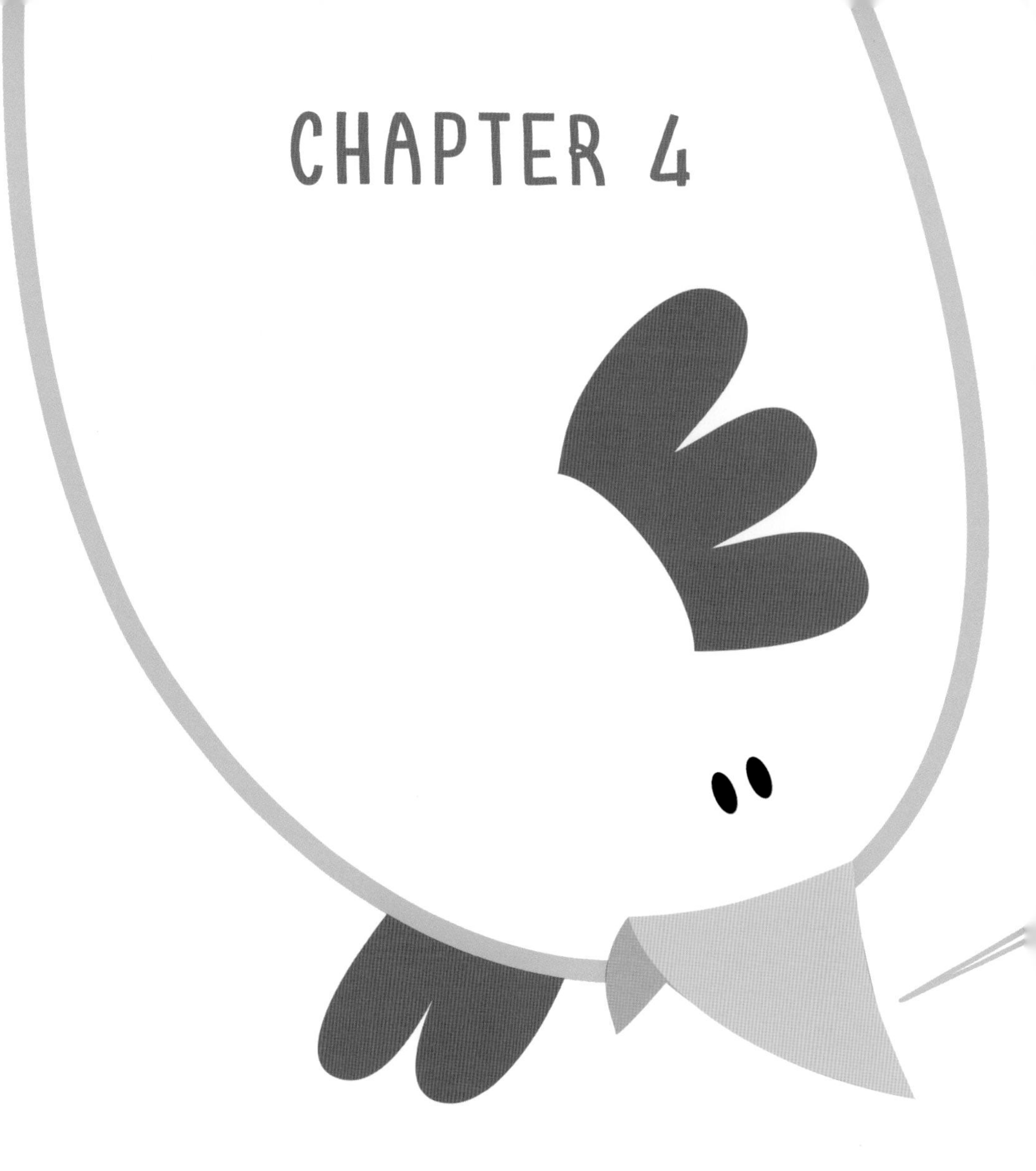

Suddenly, a fellow stepped onto the path.
His bright red hat made Snail smile.

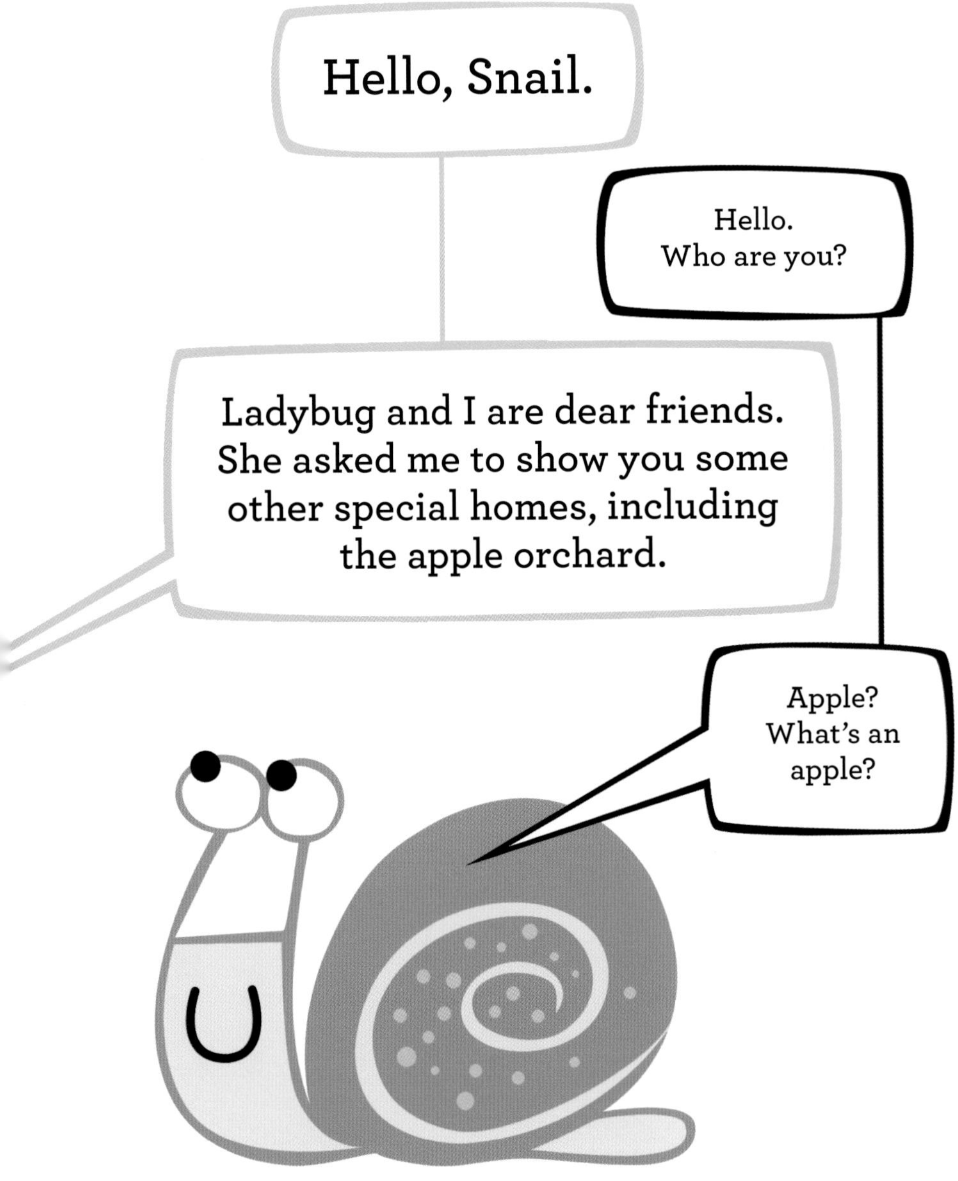
Hello, Snail.
Hello. Who are you?
Ladybug and I are dear friends. She asked me to show you some other special homes, including the apple orchard.
Apple? What's an apple?

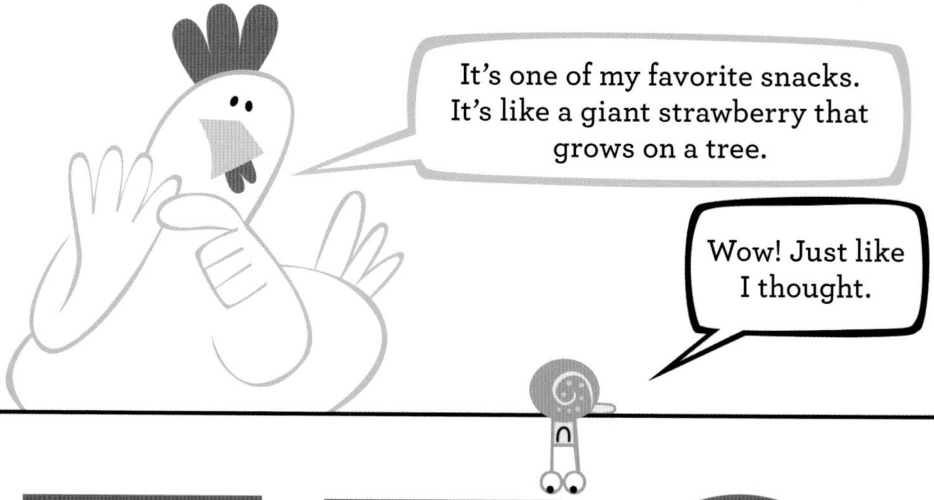
It's one of my favorite snacks. It's like a giant strawberry that grows on a tree.
Wow! Just like I thought.

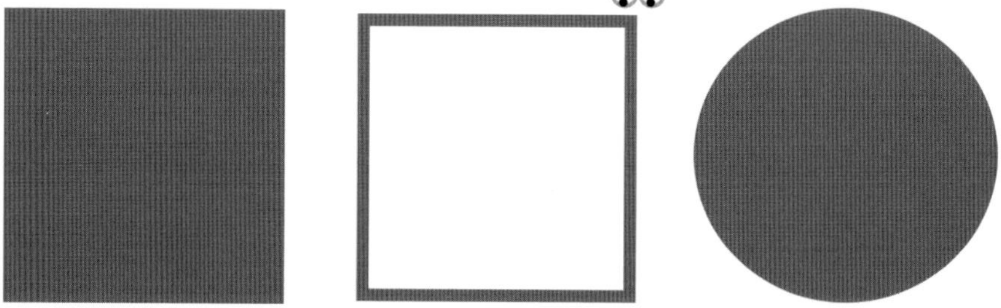

It's red on the outside,

white on the inside,

and round.

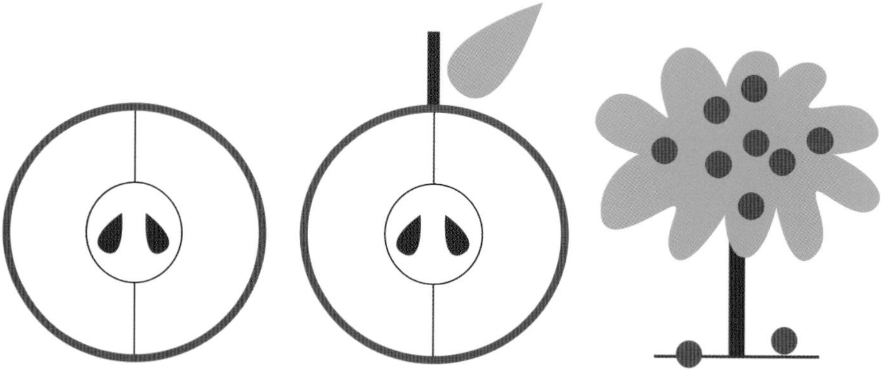

It has seeds

and a stem

and grows on trees.

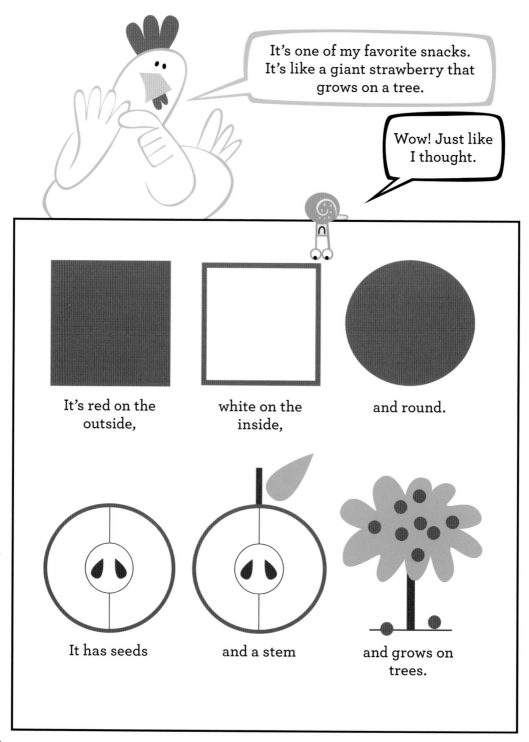

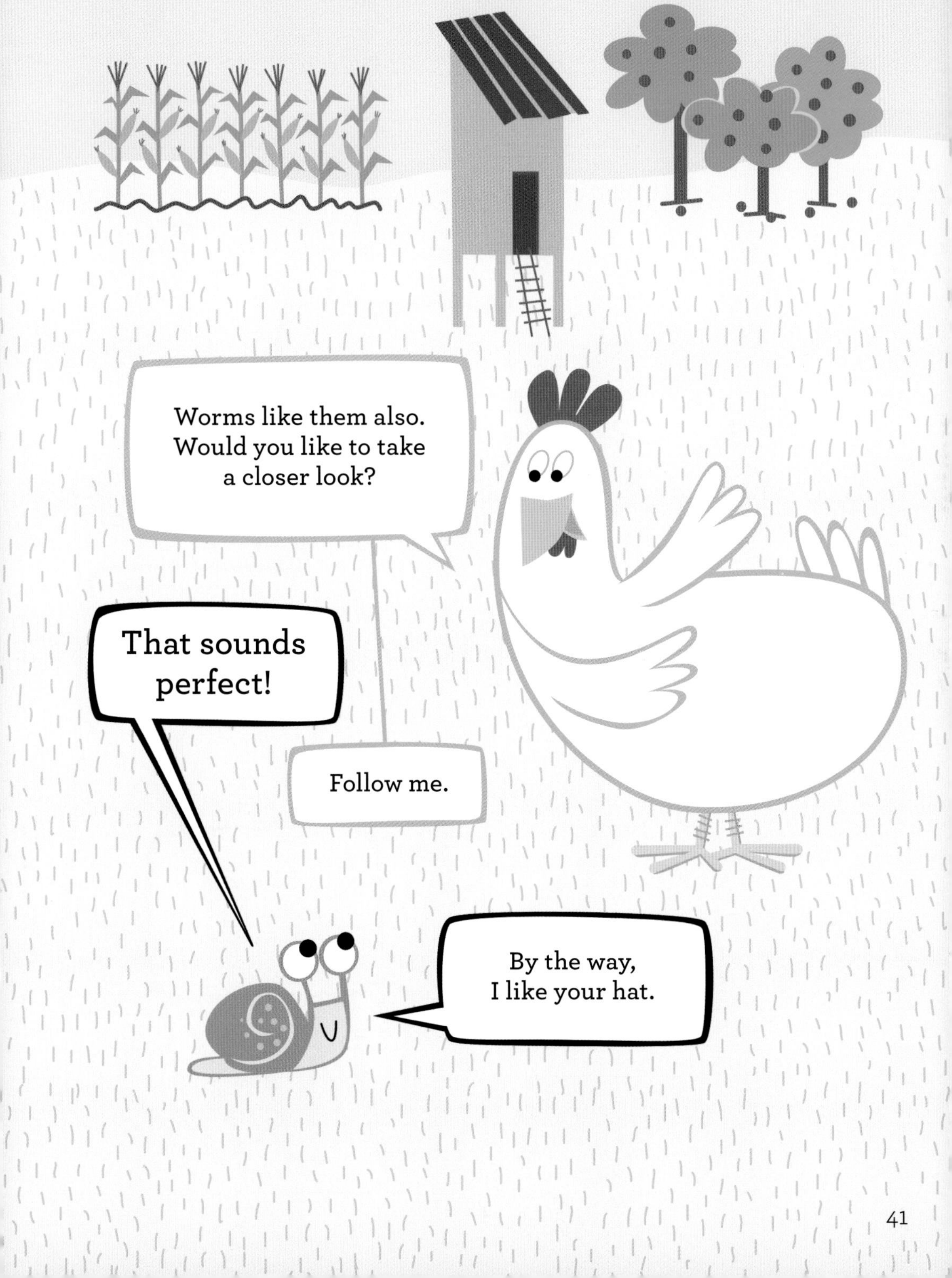
Worms like them also. Would you like to take a closer look?
That sounds perfect!
Follow me.
By the way, I like your hat.

As the search went on back at Ambrosia Acres . . .

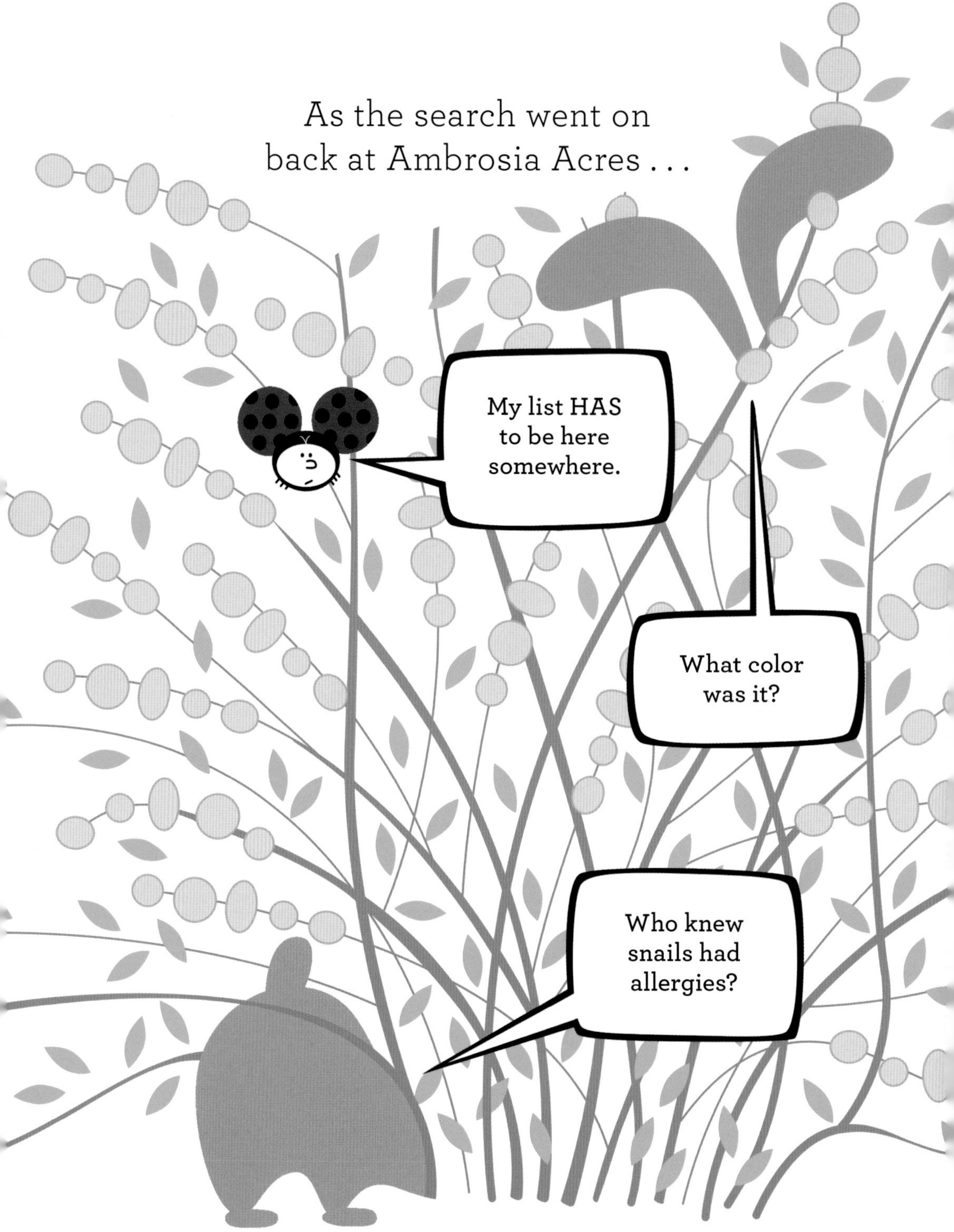
My list HAS to be here somewhere.
What color was it?
Who knew snails had allergies?

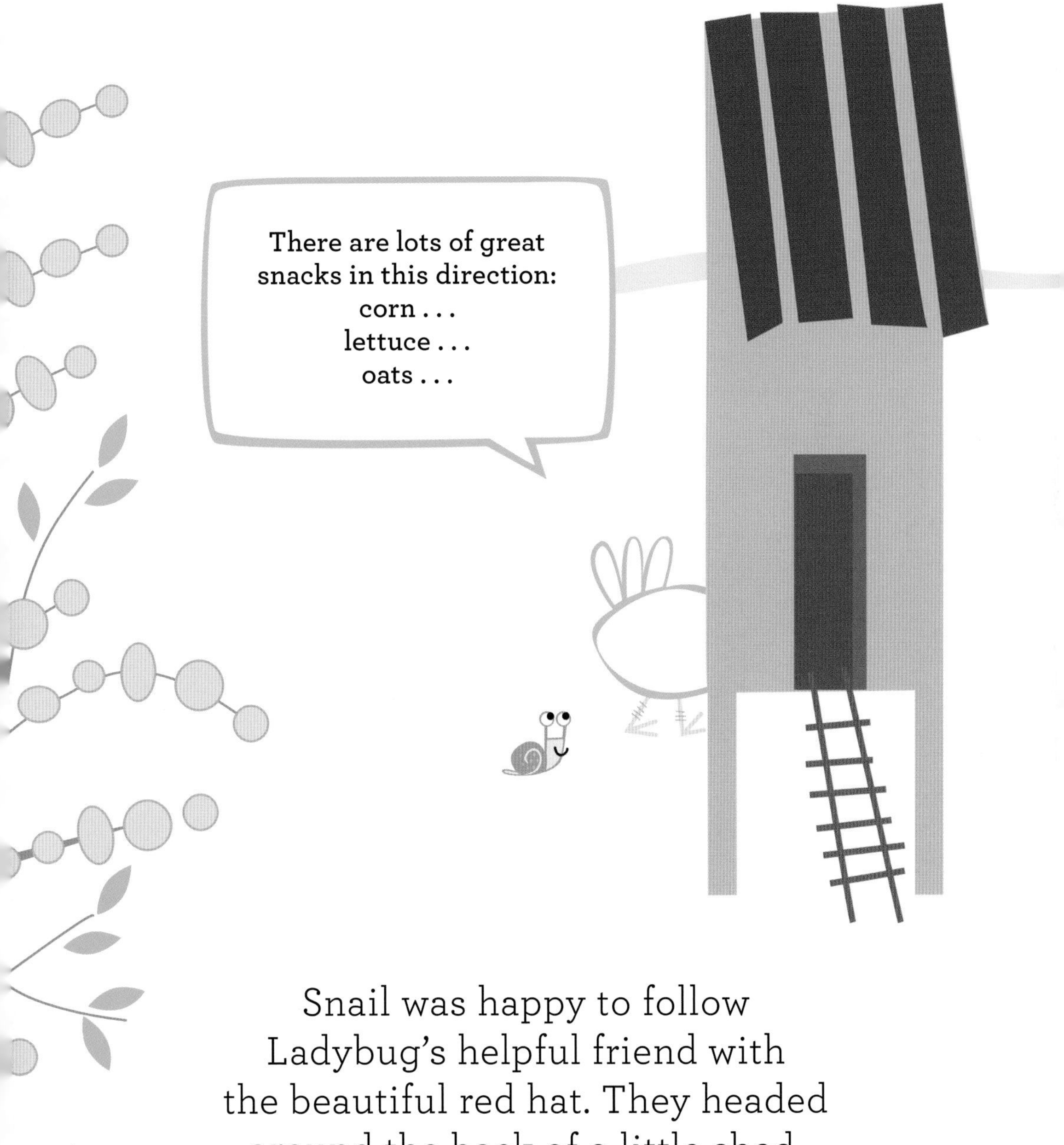
There are lots of great snacks in this direction:
corn . . .
lettuce . . .
oats . . .

Snail was happy to follow Ladybug's helpful friend with the beautiful red hat. They headed around the back of a little shed.

But when they got to the back of the shed, the fellow in the red hat stopped, causing Snail to run SMACK into his leg.

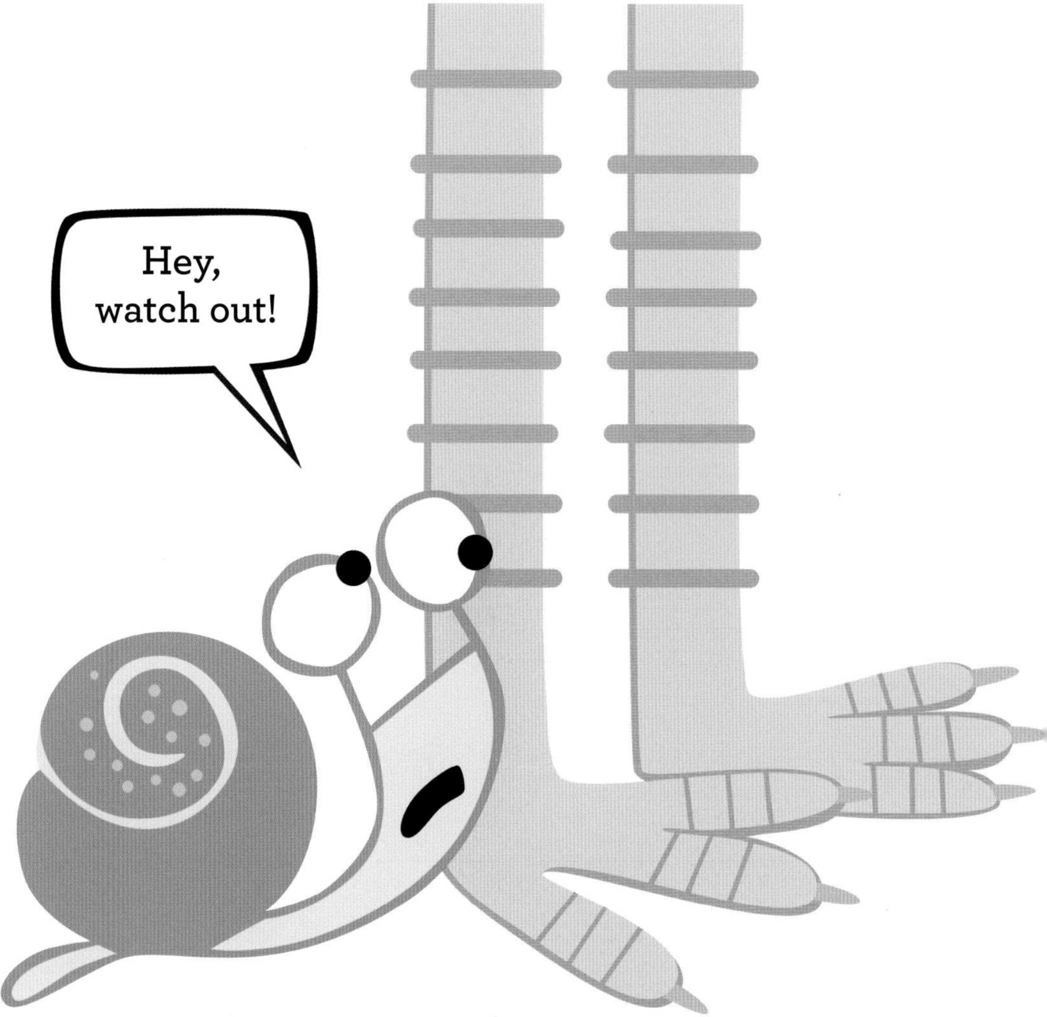
Hey, watch out!

Snail couldn't help but take a close-up look.

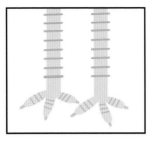

YELLOW LEGS

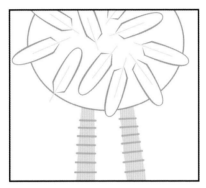

WHITE FEATHERS

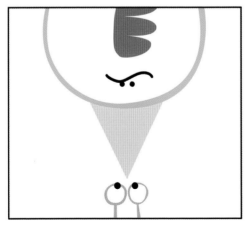

POINTY BEAK

45

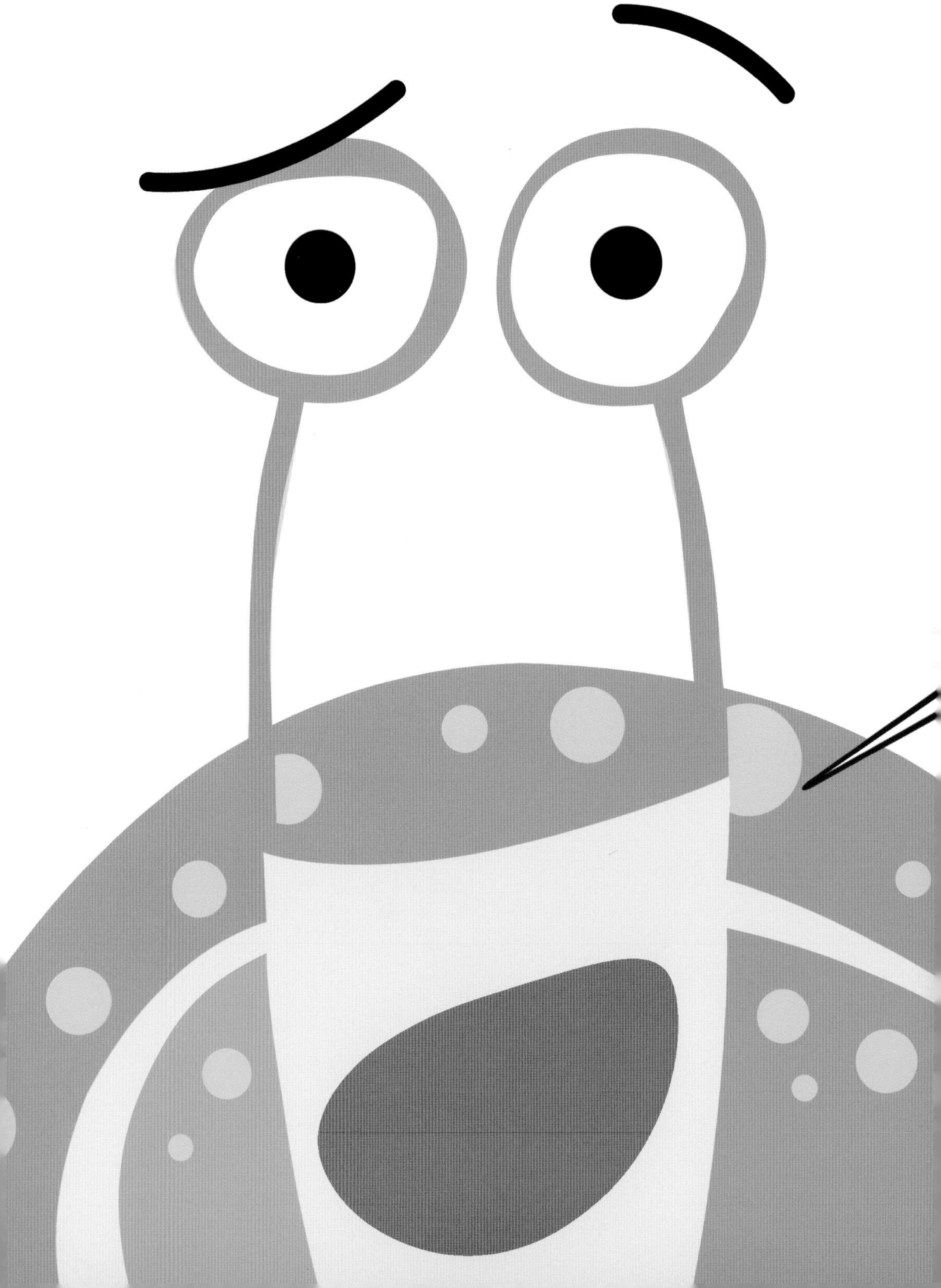

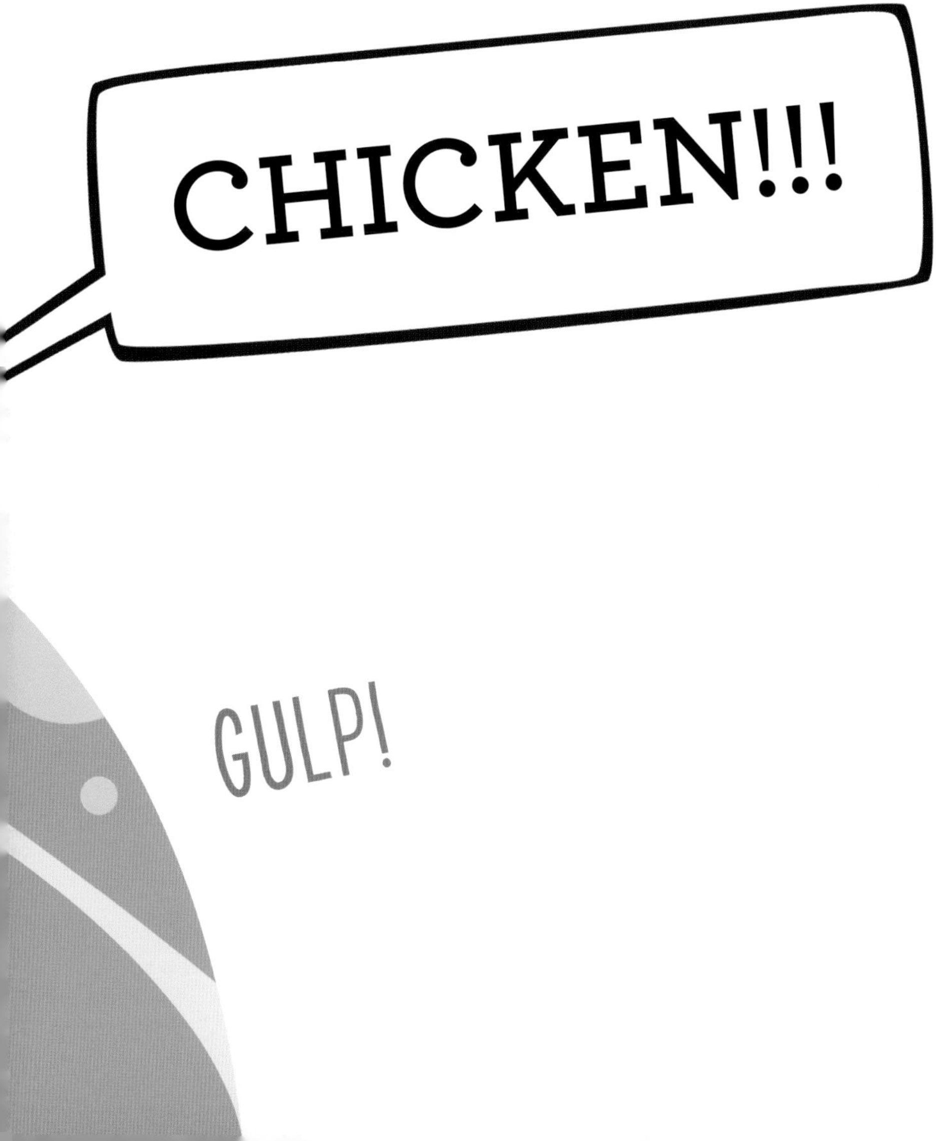
CHICKEN!!!
GULP!

Chicken grinned at Snail.

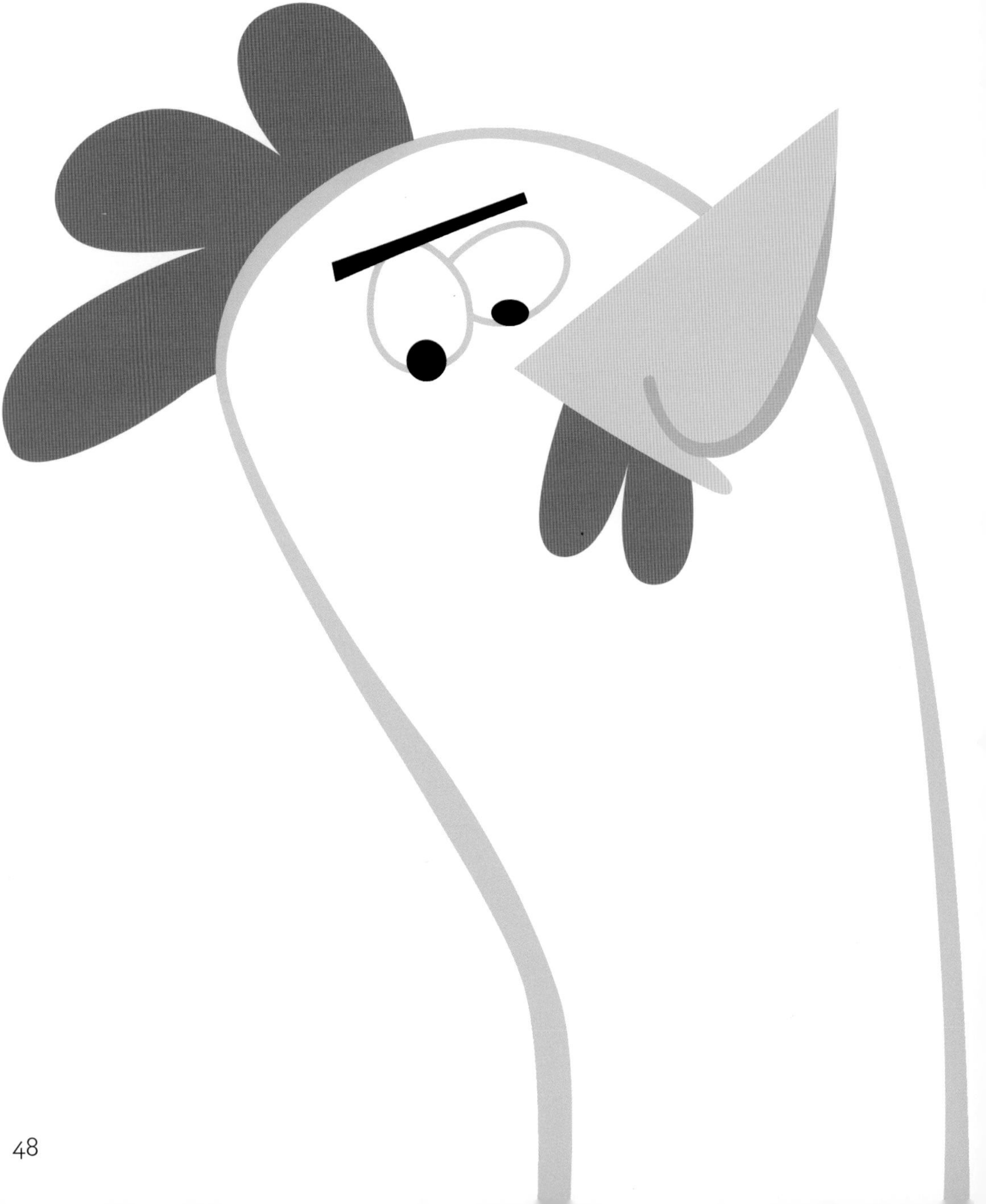

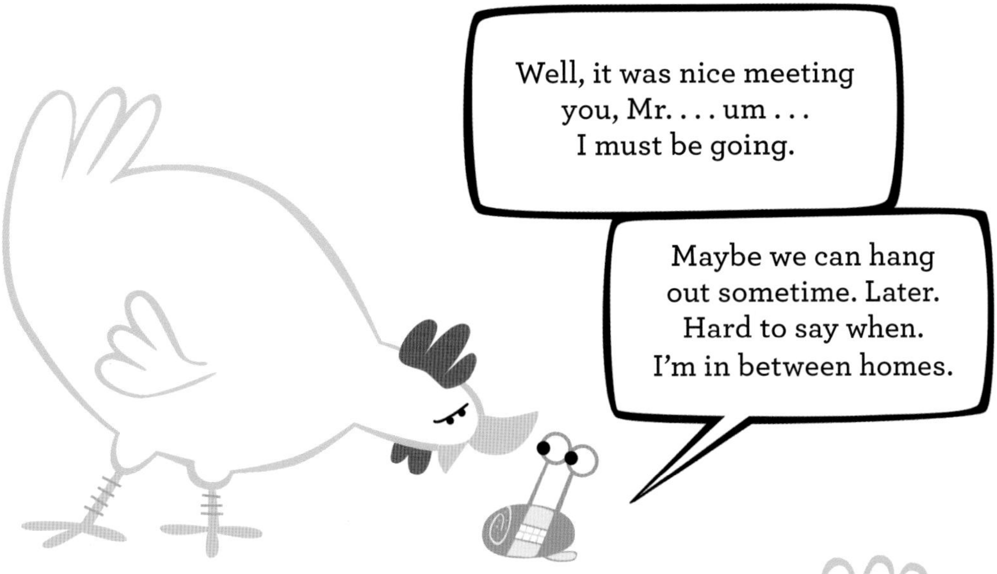
Well, it was nice meeting you, Mr. . . . um . . . I must be going.
Maybe we can hang out sometime. Later. Hard to say when. I'm in between homes.

Chicken licked his beak.

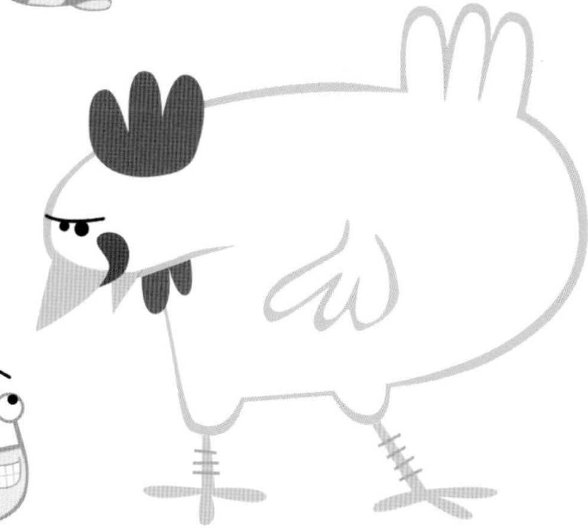

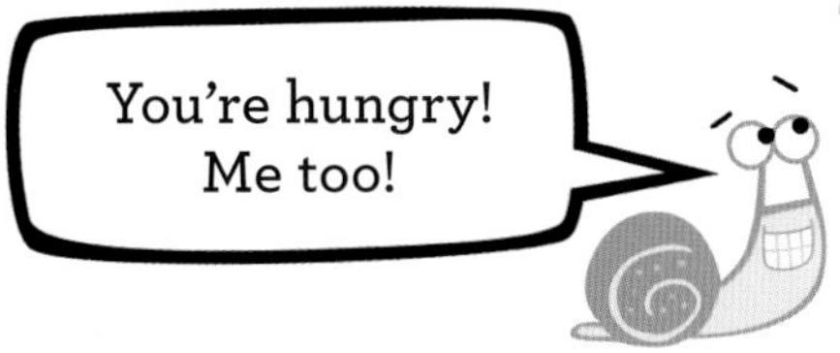
You're hungry! Me too!

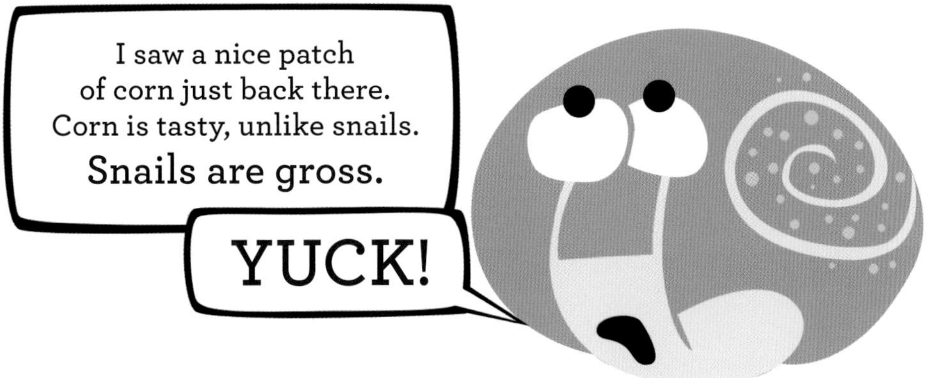
I saw a nice patch of corn just back there. Corn is tasty, unlike snails. Snails are gross.
YUCK!

Chicken leaned in close.

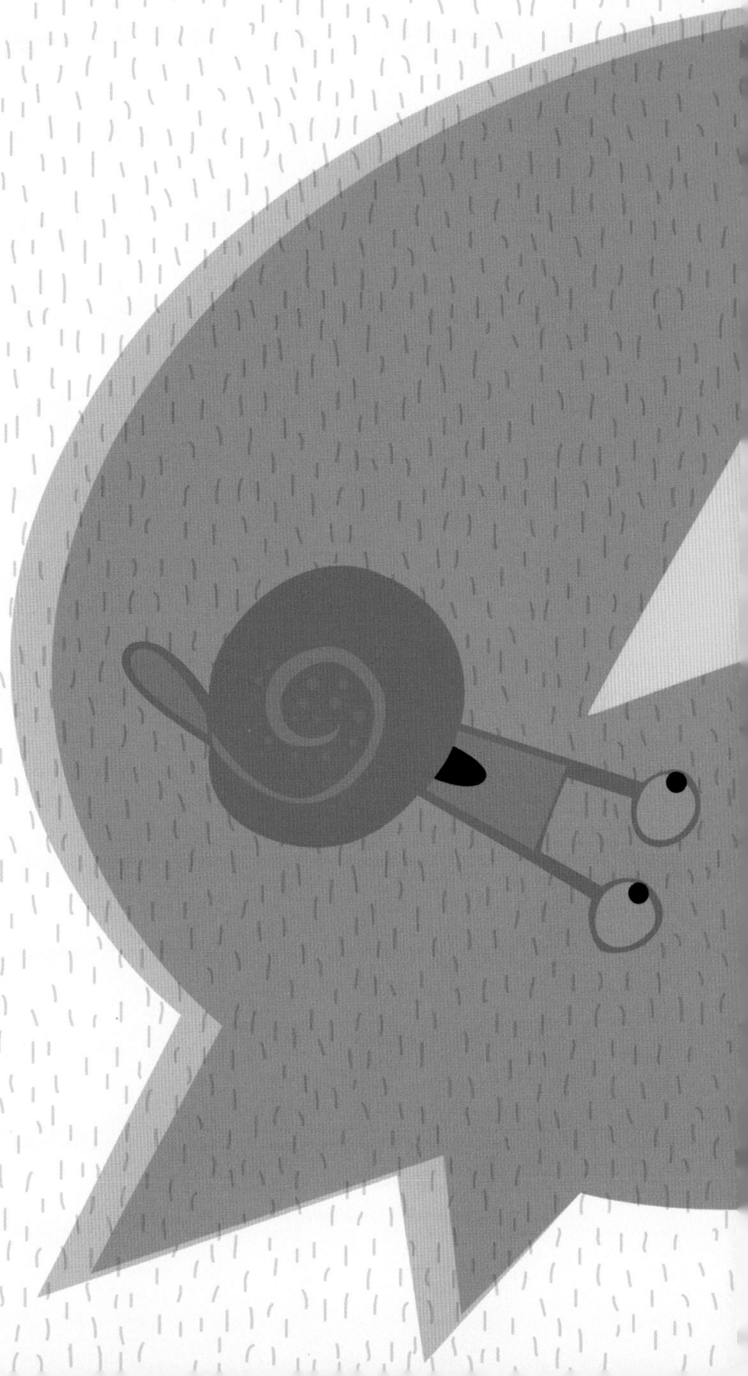

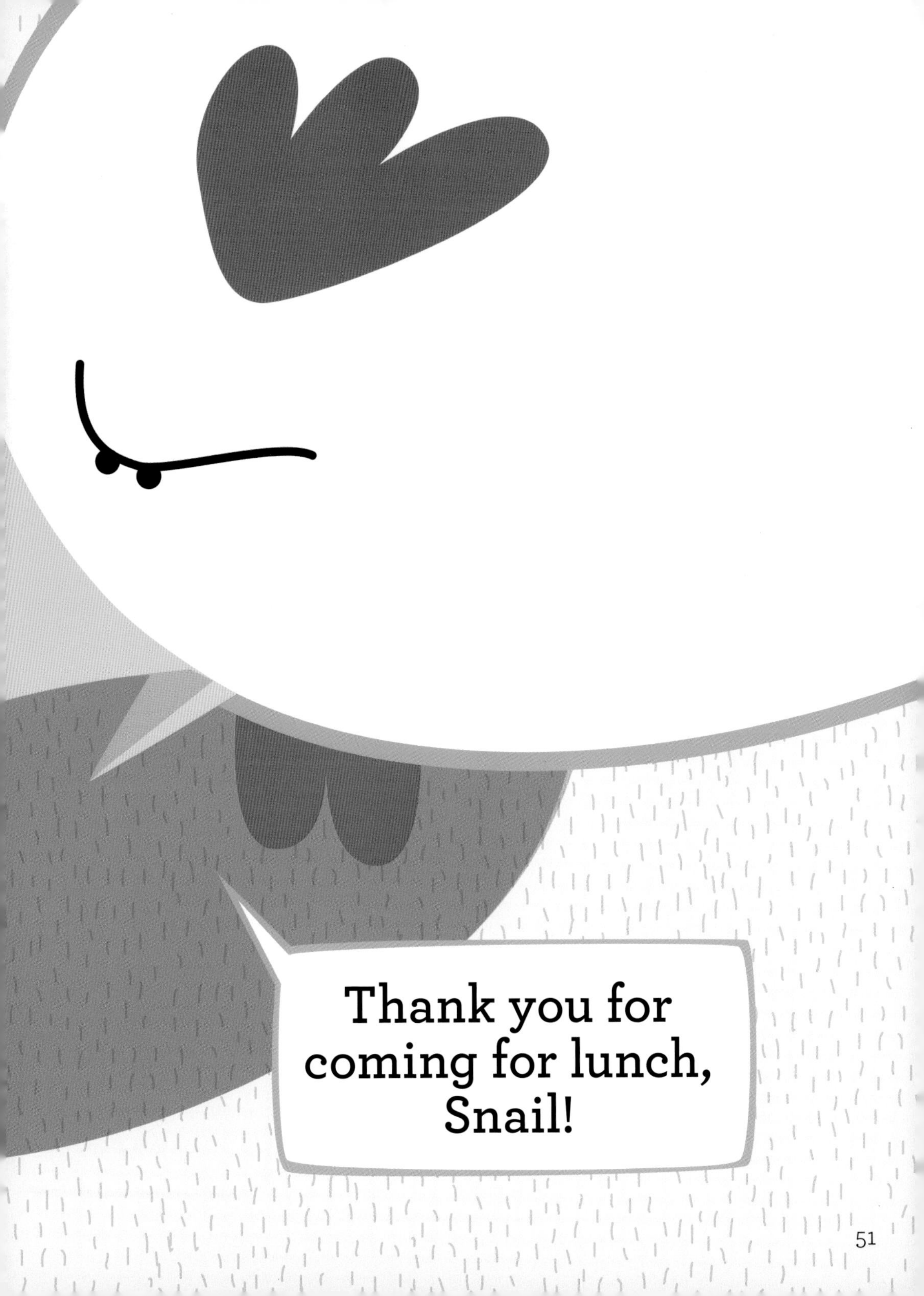
Thank you for
coming for lunch,
Snail!

Meanwhile, back at Ambrosia Acres . . .

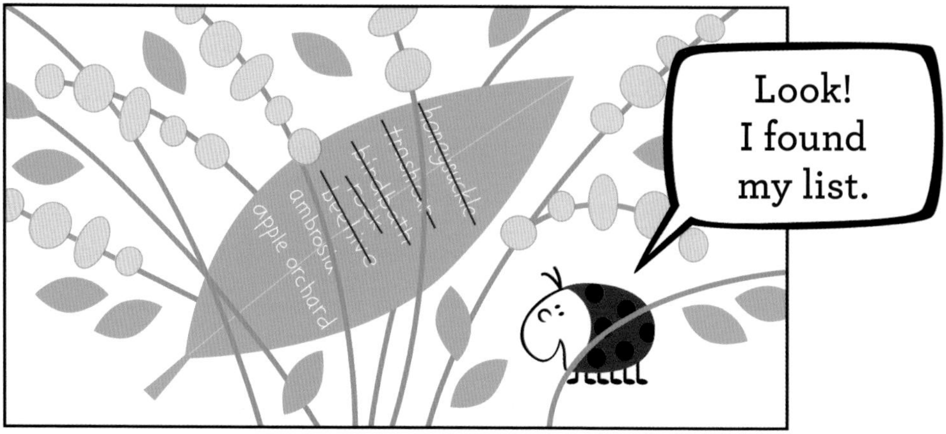
Look!
I found
my list.
ambrosia
apple orchard

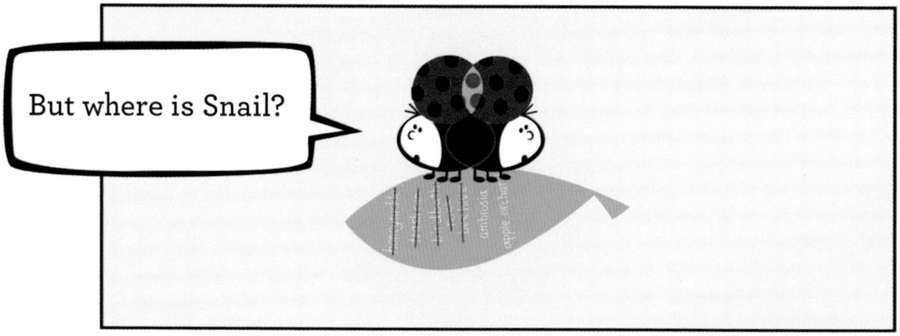
But where is Snail?

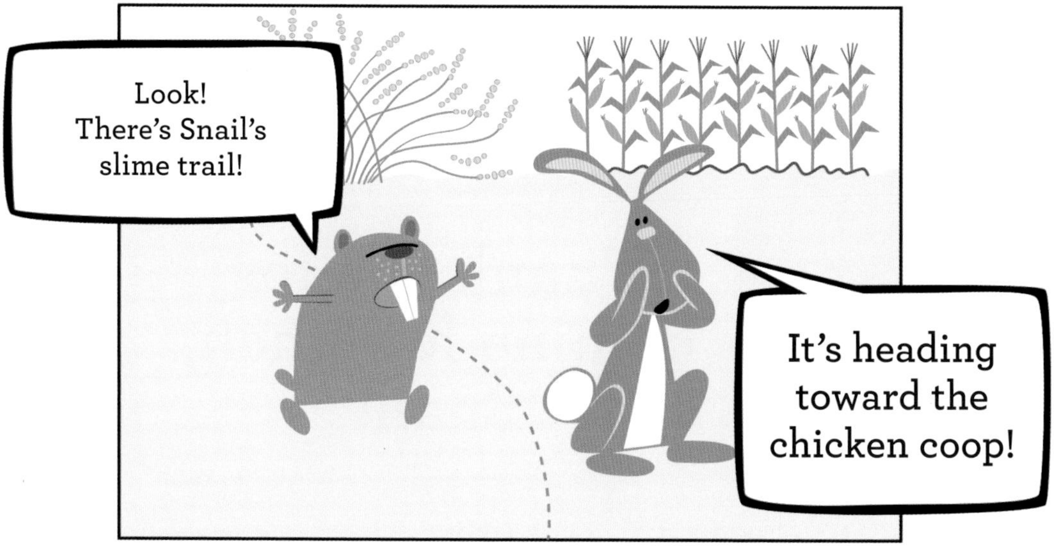
Look!
There's Snail's
slime trail!
It's heading
toward the
chicken coop!

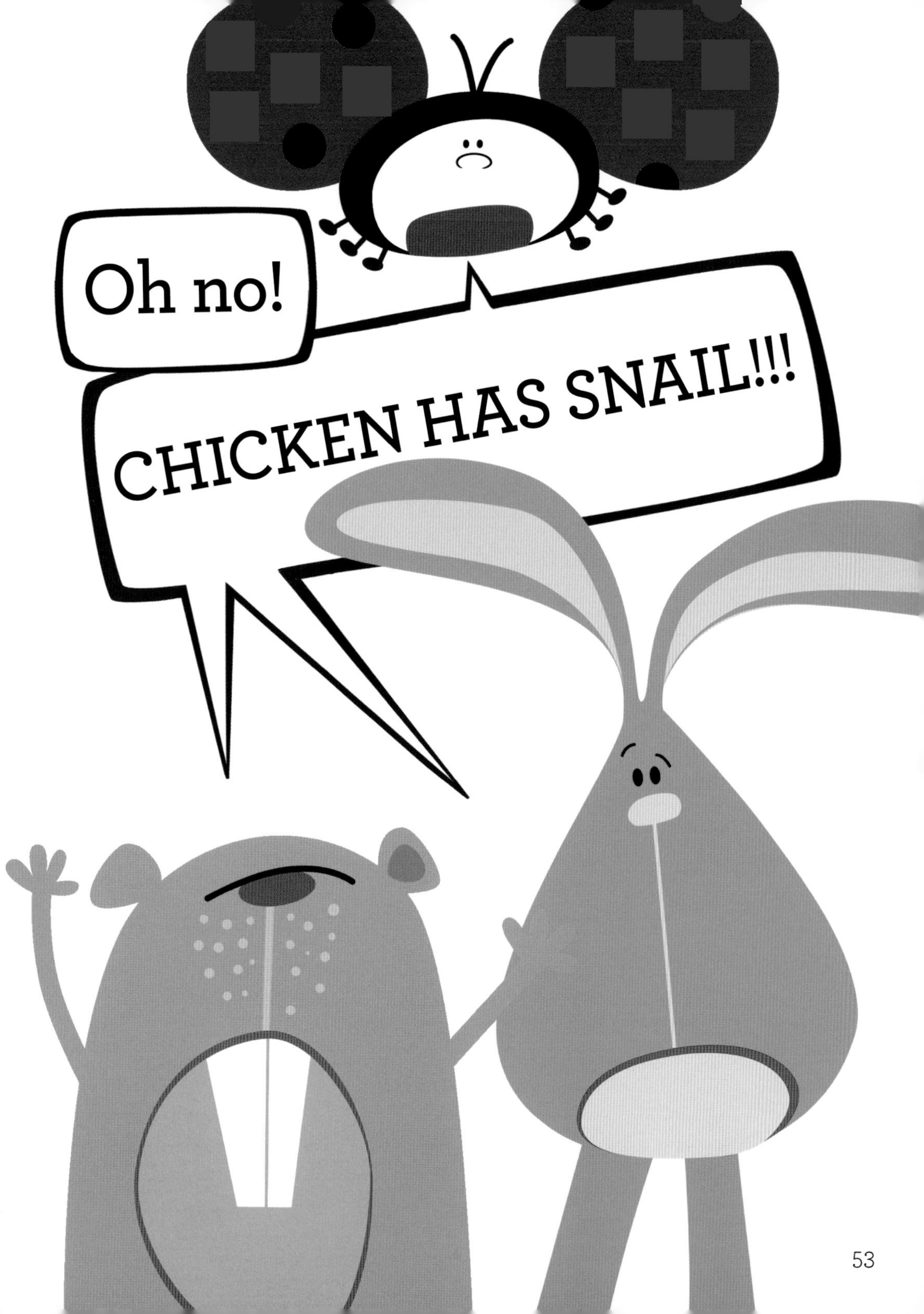
Oh no!
CHICKEN HAS SNAIL!!!

CHAPTER 5

Chicken snatched Snail into his beak.

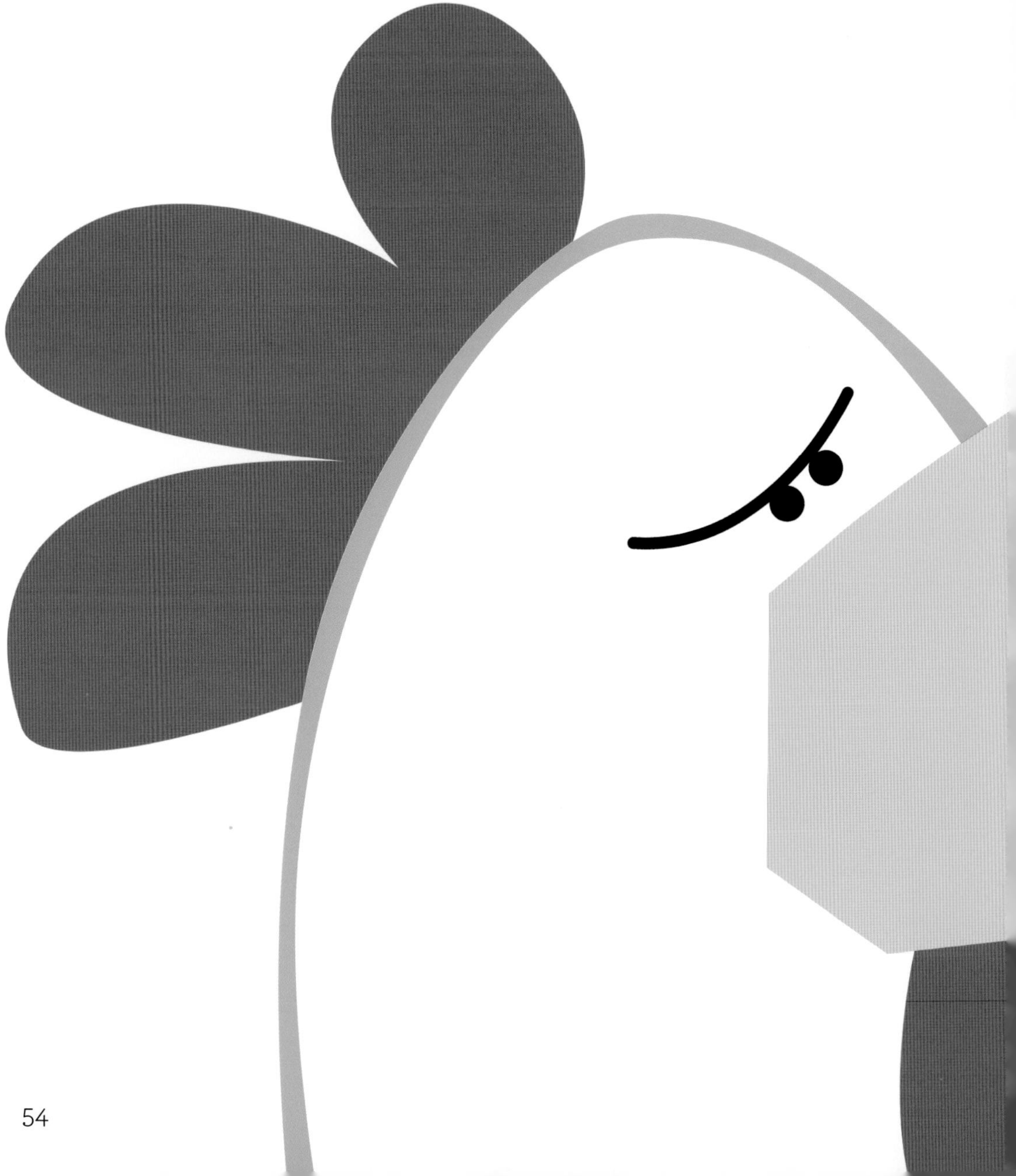

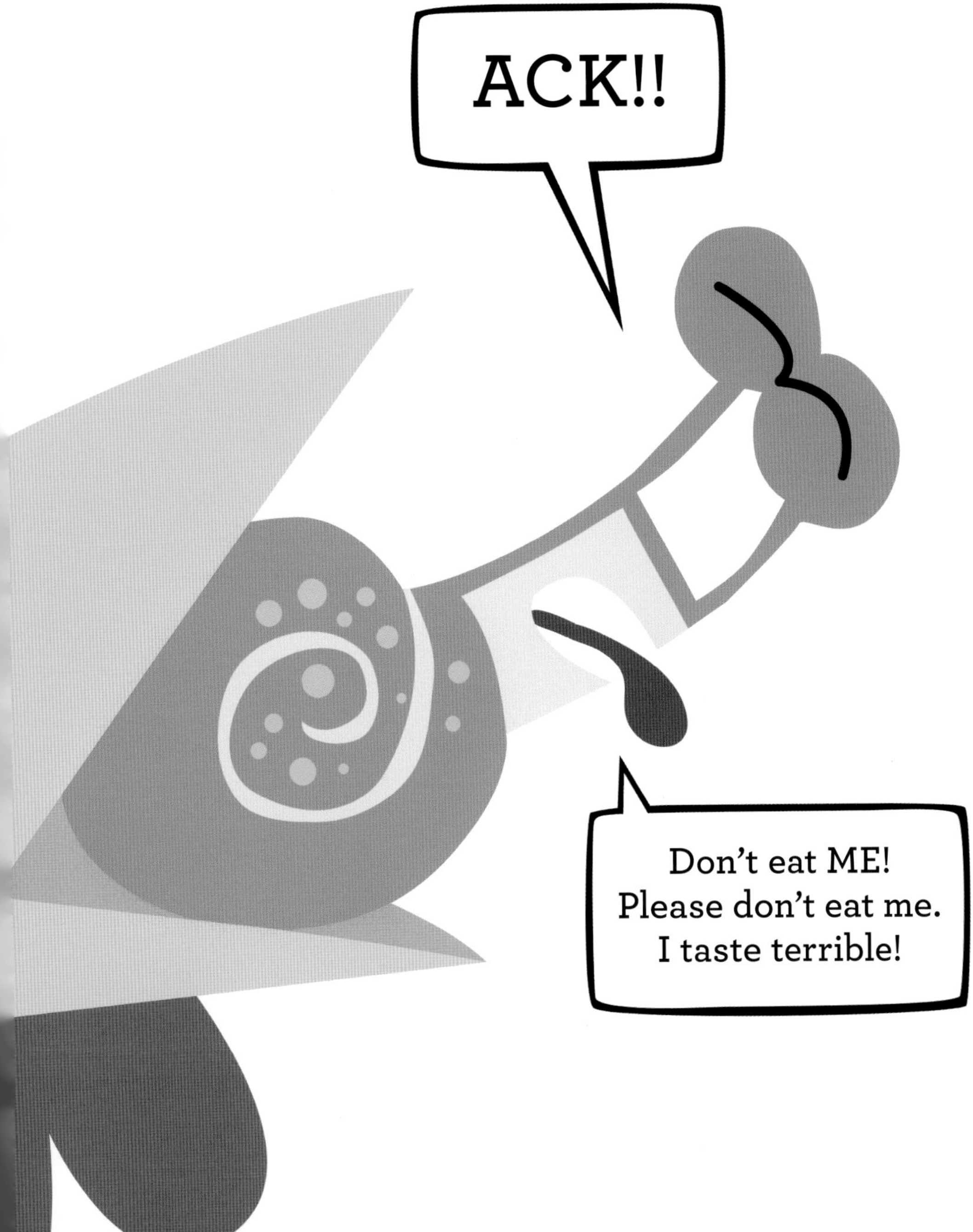
ACK!!
Don't eat ME! Please don't eat me. I taste terrible!

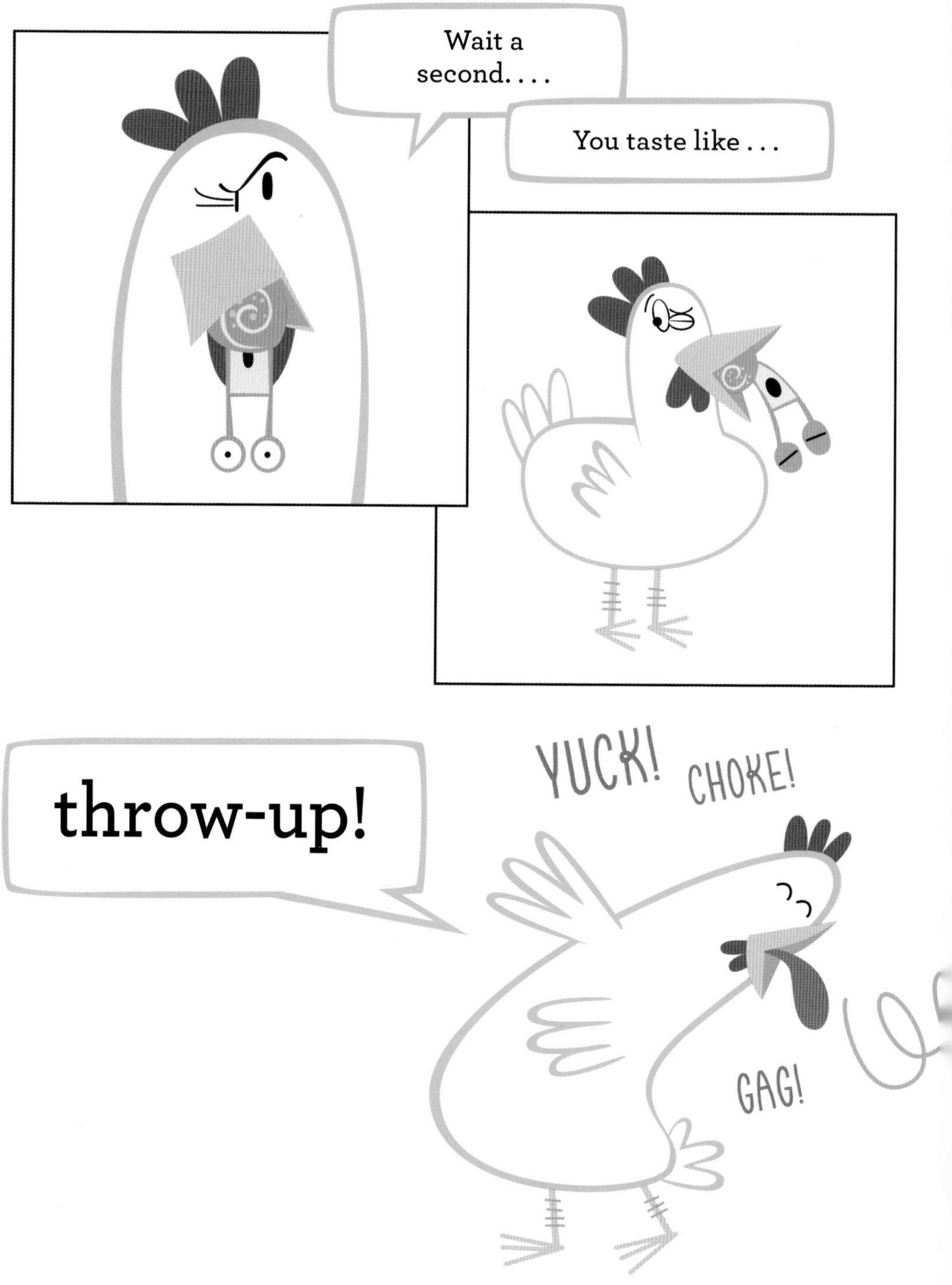
Wait a second. . . .
You taste like . . .
throw-up!
YUCK!
CHOKE!
GAG!

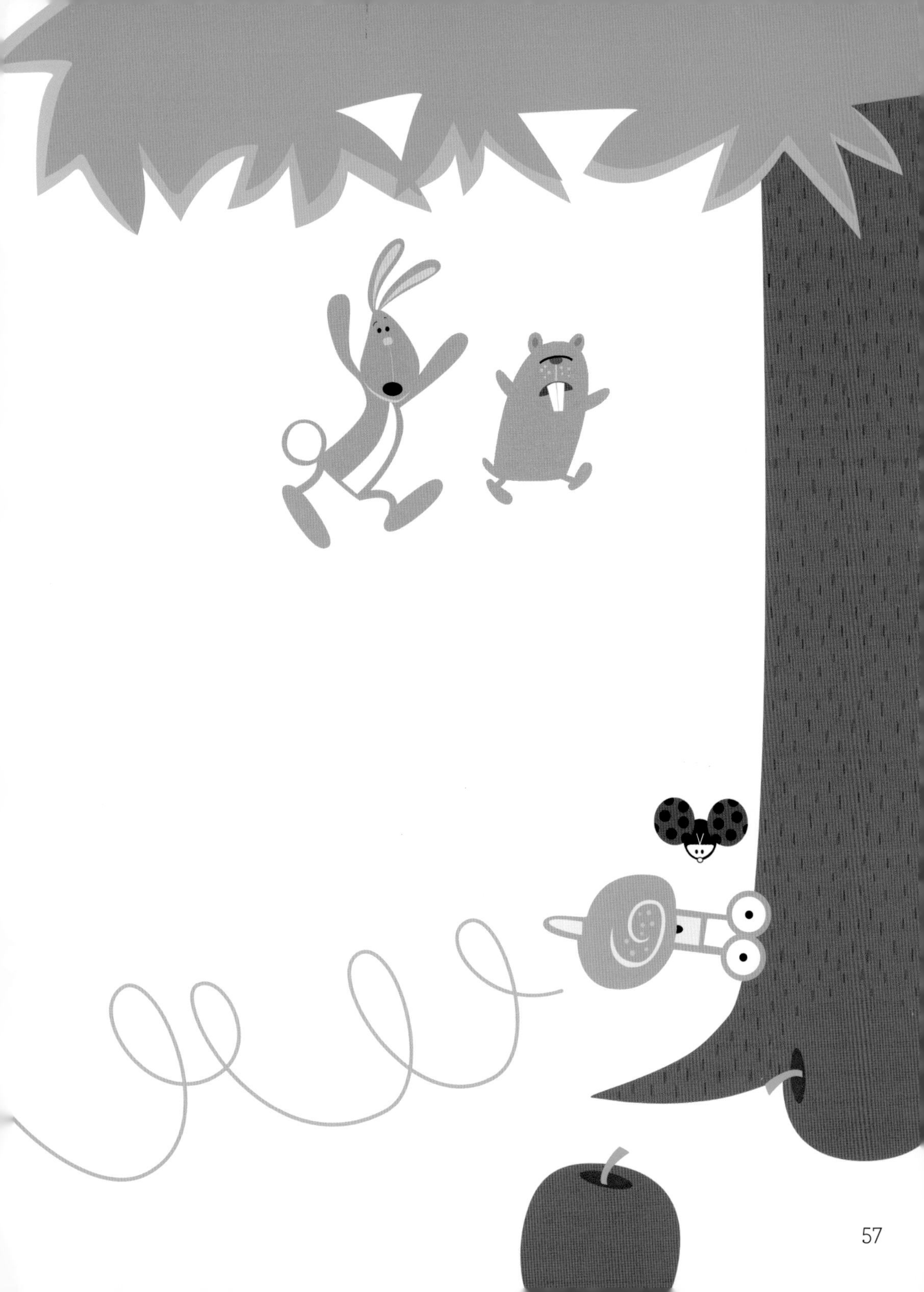

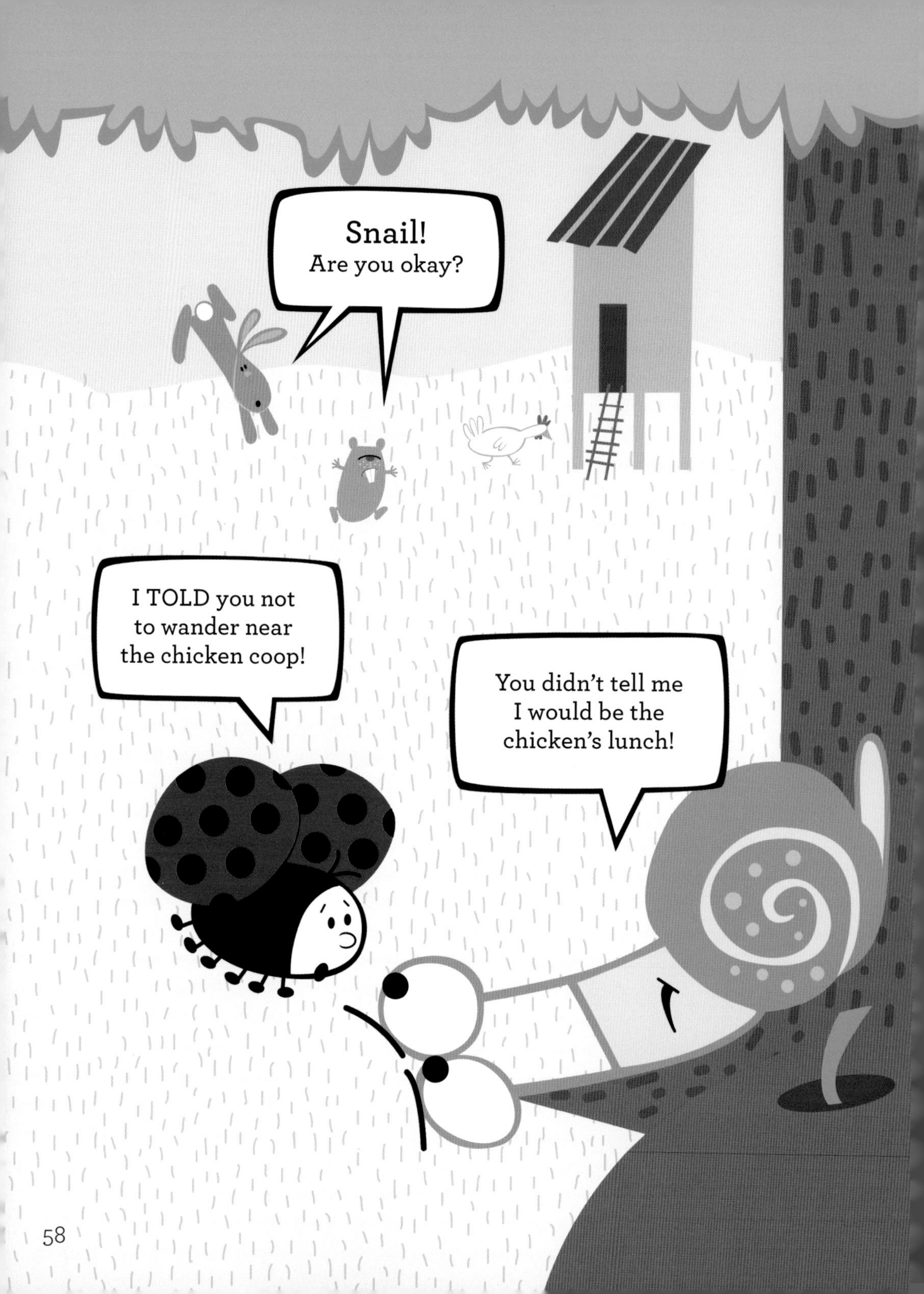
Snail! Are you okay?
I TOLD you not to wander near the chicken coop!
You didn't tell me I would be the chicken's lunch!

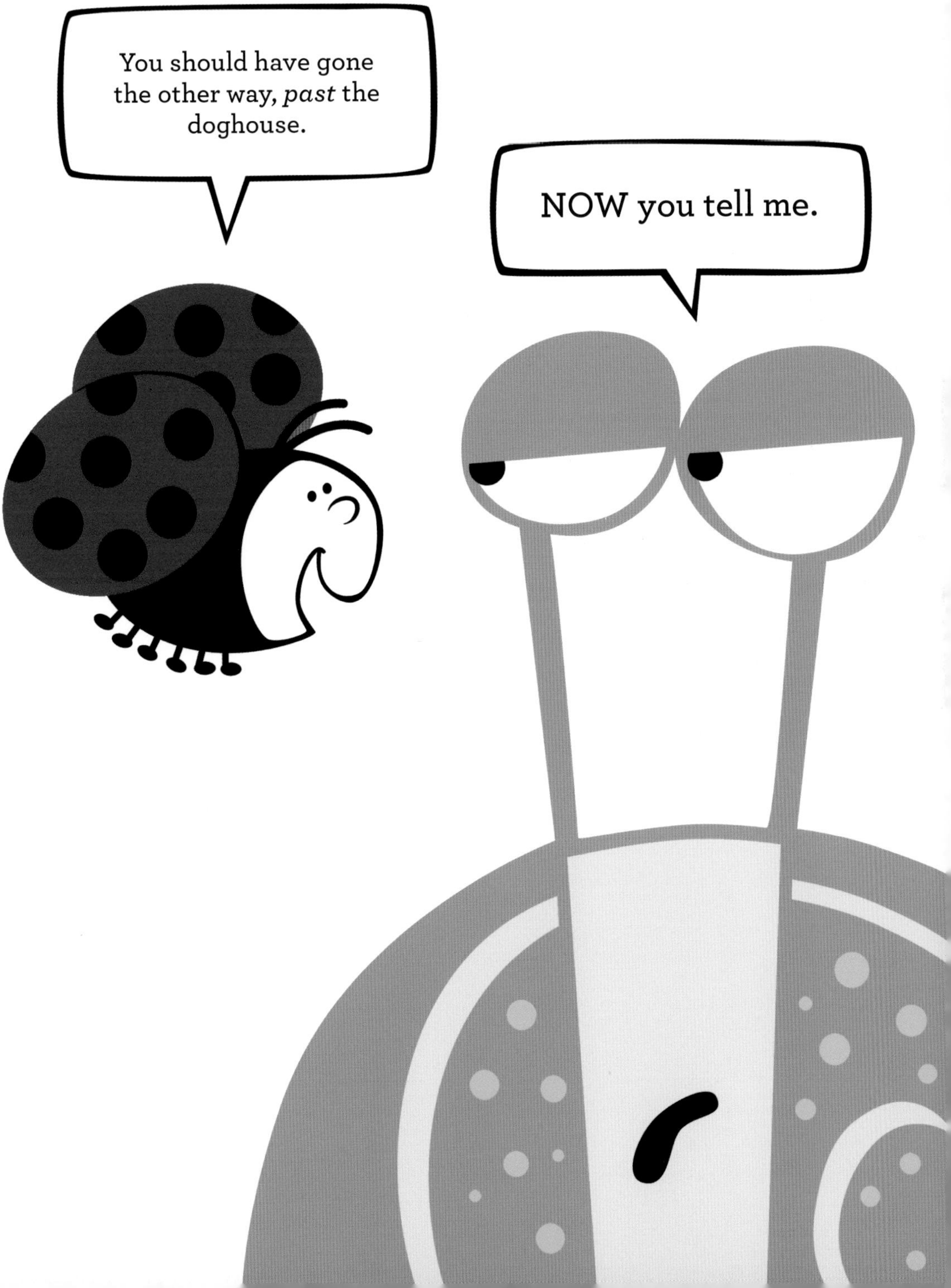
You should have gone the other way, *past* the doghouse.
NOW you tell me.

Snail couldn't stay
angry for long, because
lying next to him was
a bright red apple
on a pile of brown
grass and dirt.

Snail couldn't
help himself.

He took a bite.

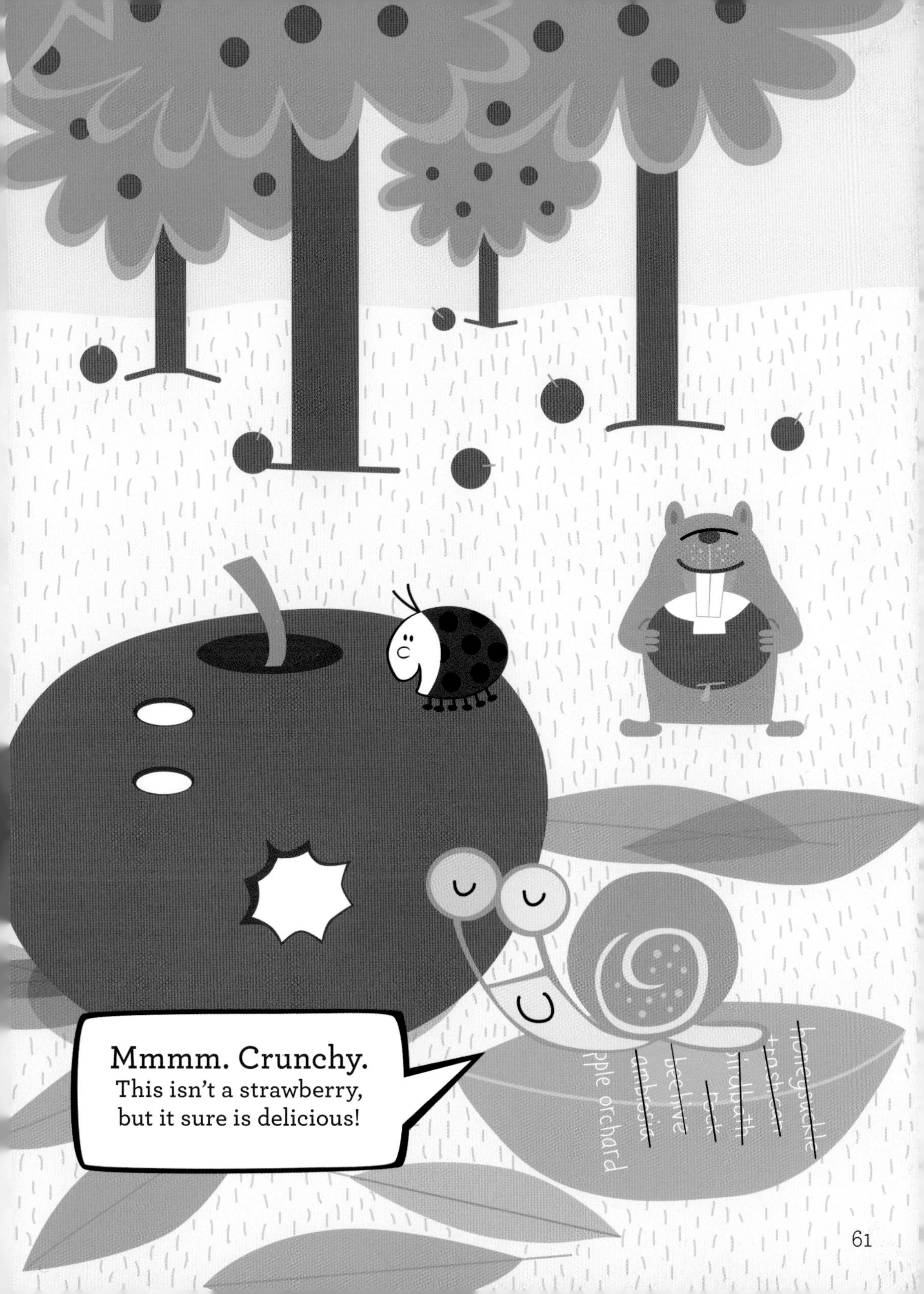
Mmmm. Crunchy.
This isn’t a strawberry, but it sure is delicious!

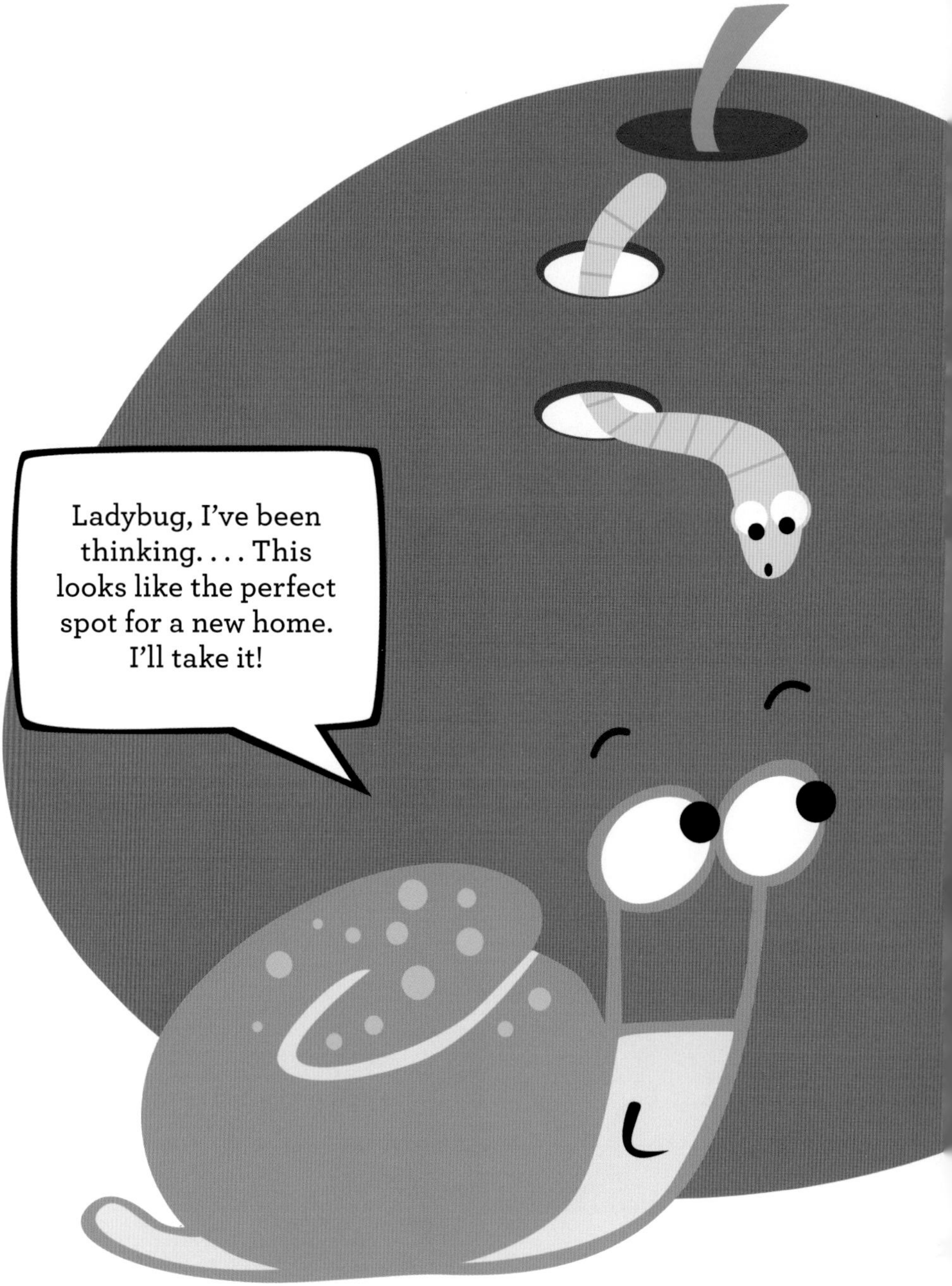
Ladybug, I've been thinking. . . . This looks like the perfect spot for a new home. I'll take it!

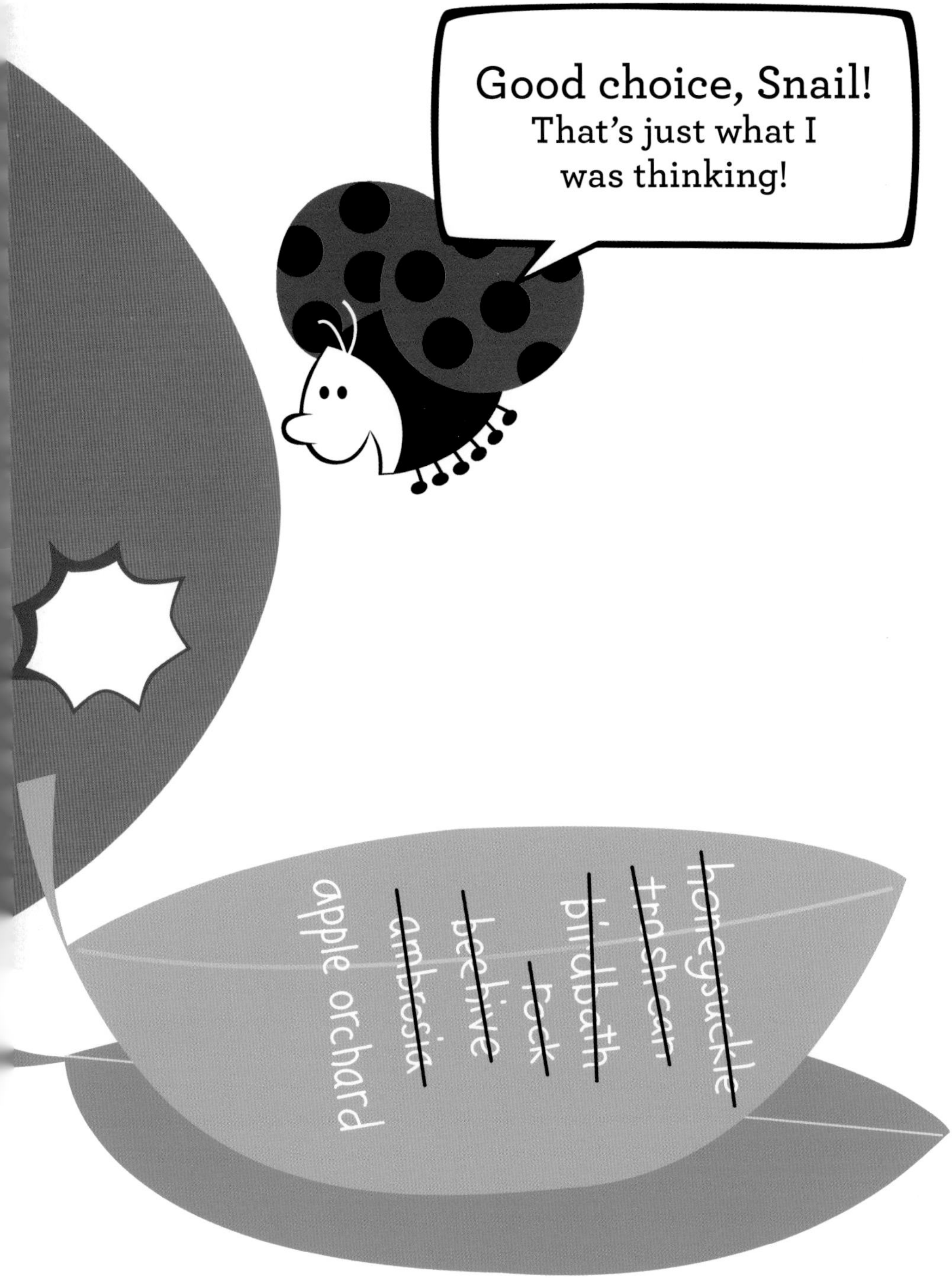
Good choice, Snail!
That's just what I was thinking!
~~honeysuckle~~
~~trash can~~
~~birdbath~~
~~rock~~
~~beehive~~
~~ambrosia~~
apple orchard

Mary Peterson is an illustrator of many books for young readers, including *Dig In!*, *Piggies in the Pumpkin Patch*, *Wiggle and Waggle*, *Wooby & Peep*, and *Snail Has Lunch*. She lives in Los Angeles, California.